Legend of the Lost

Ian P Buckingham

Green Cat Books

SECOND EDITION
Published in 2020 by
GREEN CAT BOOKS
19 St Christopher's Way
Pride Park
Derby
DE24 8JY
www.green-cat.co

ISBN: 978-1-913794-05-7

First published in Great Britain in 2018
by The Book Guild Ltd

Legend of the Lost

For Holly and Alice Buckingham, our own heroic duo.
You were the creative inspiration
and wind beneath the wings of this series.
You helped me remember that children's books are never a fantasy
if we all keep believing.

Contents

Foreword

One of the decisions a writer has to make, especially when creating characters never shared before, is whether to include pictures or illustrations.

I have chosen not to in the first book as I believe it is important for my readers to blend my words with their imaginations to visualise the characters, creatures and places. Your mind is where the magic really happens, as you know.

However, we have created a special range of online places for inquisitive brains and curious folk who would like to explore the *Legend of the Lost* in more detail and perhaps share thoughts and ideas with others.

We will be posting bonus material from the author, puzzles, quizzes and advance notices of forthcoming events as well as unique extracts from the next book in the series, *The Ends of the Earth*.

Simply connect with us on one of these sites and just mention who your favourite character is, for exclusive access.

Fans of the *Legend of the Lost* saga are most welcome to join us via:

Twitter: @ConnectLOL
Facebook: Legend of The Lost
Instagram: connectwithlotl

Book 1

The Moonstone and Rubyrobe

Holly gasped.

The sweat was flowing, running into her eyes, burning as she ran.

Lungs screamed, heavy, horribly dry.

She gulped down hot air, chest heaving with terror.

She could hear herself crying in panic – "Faster, run faster," – and she could feel the fine hairs, taut all over her body, prickling with fear.

She clawed through the mud and threw herself between the dark roots of an ancient tree.

Yet still the thud, thud, thud of the footsteps came.

They were relentless, like a pack of rabid horrors on the hunt.

And they were chasing her through the dark woods that everyone had told her to avoid at all costs.

But now it was too late.

She was on her own.

They were coming for her.

They were here…

Just two days earlier, the Savage clan had woken to dappled golden seaside sunlight streaming in through the bay window of the impossibly pretty Mermaid Cottage.

The smell of freshly baked bacon butties filled the air, as it did every morning of their holiday, while excited seagull shrieks drowned out Dad's dull radio.

"There they go," said Dad, "pebble-dashing the car again."

Holly and her sister Lucy giggled. They still weren't sure what "pebble dashed" meant but they knew it was rude. Most of all they enjoyed watching their dad chase the birds away, only for them to settle on their roof rack again as soon as his back was turned, laughing like they were teasing him.

Nanna Jo shuffled in, her face buried in the local newspaper, and announced, "I knew it! It's beachcombing Saturday this weekend, girls."

"Arrrrhhhh," said Dad, pretending to be a pirate, badly. "Thas yr wall be dagin up treasure, sure we shall."

The girls fell about shrieking as he chased them round the room, hopping on one leg, hunching his back and tossing a tea towel over his shoulder to form a makeshift parrot.

"Well, we may not have found as much as most in recent years, but we wouldn't have the Moonstone if we hadn't searched those rock pools, now would we?"

A shadow passed fleetingly over Dad's face as Nanna Jo opened the top of the stable-style doors that led from the kitchen; she couldn't help but smile, as she always did when talking about their now-famous "magical" archway.

Family and friends had collected the "found things" that decorated the arch above their bright yellow front door.

Emerald, sapphire and ruby sea glass worn smooth by the waves and, as they liked to imagine, the fond caresses of mythical sea folk were set into the stone next to silver and pearl-white shells.

Once-colourful starfish appeared here and there along with bright red and jet-black stones, perfect spheres that Dad said were a little bit radioactive. They were the "danger rocks", as little Lucy had called them ever since she could talk.

Twisted and tangled driftwood picked out the outline of the arch.

Mock seaweed trails decorated the bumpy plaster.

But, in pride of place, at the pointy pinnacle of the uppermost triangle right above the cottage door, was the now-famous, milky-white stone that flashed with rainbow hues in all of the different kinds of light they got here on the south-west coast at the tip of ancient Britain.

"It's so pretty," sighed Holly, her arm around her Nanna's waist, eyes twinkling.

"Yes," she smiled. "It is, m'dear. And Saturday night is the first time we'll see it when the moon is at its best."

"Will the fairies come again?" asked Lucy. She famously loved all things with wings, especially the glittery things. "And their magical friends?"

Everybody laughed, including the little redhead, whose face slowly turned the colour of her slightly curly locks.

Everybody, that is, apart from Nanna Jo, who simply smiled, with a knowing twinkle, and slowly polished the warm mist of her breath from the translucent stone with the palm of her outstretched hand.

"Who knows, Lu Lu? Who knows, m'love?"

Mermaid Cottage nestled snugly in a terraced row of brightly coloured houses that lined Porthleven harbour.

Each house was painted in its own unique style that gave the harbourside a lovely Liquorice Allsorts style.

The seaside town's famous seafront was a popular pet-exercising promenade for local Cornish folk and holidaymakers alike. It was a favourite spot for long lazy walks or storm-watching along Smuggler's Row. There, the waves were known to break right over the tall clock tower, which could be seen for many coastal miles.

Although the sun twinkled peacefully on the flat, gently ebbing water today, like an inviting, refreshing pool, even someone of Holly's ten tender years was very aware that the sea could be spiteful at times.

A plaque on the harbour wall recalled an infamous storm at the turn of the century that claimed the lives of two local policemen. They had been swept down to the dark deep in their panda car, lights still flashing. It was an image that, once in your mind, it was hard to forget.

Another sign, in the ancient smuggler's Ship Inn pub that served the "tastiest fish and chips on the Lizard", told the story of a shipwreck that claimed the lives of a whole family on the same dismal winter's night.

Holly had often thought about those poor, faceless folk.

She and Lucy sometimes built sand people on the beach, dressed with lost flip flops, bits of bottles, fishing line and other high-tide flotsam in tribute to the shipwrecked souls, long before they really understood the tragedy. They even gave them names.

But then, as always, the high tide would return and the waves would claim them all over again.

It was during beach play dates like these, often with their friends Reanna, Alex and Niamh, whose families also holidayed here and who loved to build castles or comb the rock pools, bursting with wriggly life, that they sometimes found the treasures for their famous cottage doorway.

Because of their collection of shiny things, you could usually spot their house, across the bay, glistening in the summer sunlight. Over the years the smiling sun had gradually bleached the Mermaid Cottage driftwood and slate sign.

The moment they found the Moonstone last year wasn't any special sort of a day, just another long and lovely afternoon spent rock pooling down at nearby Coverack beach.

Nestled amid the blue-and-yellow striped cushions, Holly cast her mind back to how the usual excited groups of families had gathered in a multicoloured straggle of smiling strangers hoping to speed up low tide.

Just as soon as enough soggy sand was showing, they had set off armed with buckets, spades and nets, as they always did, to find the pretend "pirate hoard" discreetly hidden by the friendly team from the National Trust.

This ritual was as popular a part of the holiday calendar as the sandcastle competition, especially with the tourists. But, although they knew the best spots to look and had often won on sheer quantity of finds, the girls had never found anything particularly special in the past.

It was Holly, of course, who found the stone last year. Her pops had always said that she had special powers of brave intuition.

Others (usually her sister) just called her a bit bossy and headstrong. They were, of course, wrong.

Holly had been searching a stretch of rock pools she'd investigated many times before and was casually admiring a collection of bright purple anemones when she first spotted something glinting under a rock shelf, just below the water line.

When she reached her hand out to touch it, taking care not to attract the attentions of a grumpy crab, the stone had frightened her at first because it tingled as her hand got close. It wasn't a stingy tingle, more like touching a hot cup on a really cold day.

But it was an odd feeling at first and she pulled her arm away, sending the surrounding tentacled ladies scurrying back into their simple green huts as if they had been guilty.

Yet something nagged at her to persist, to reach through the water again. And then, after a few brief moments of sifting with her hands, she was holding up an object both dull and beautiful. It gleamed against the sun and drew her companions to her, who gathered round, all excited.

"Oooh," said Reanna. "Is that a pearl? Did the National Trust Team hide it for us to find?"

"No," said Niamh. "It's a precious stone, I think."

"Don't be silly," said Lucy. "It's been left by a faerie, of course."

But as the girls giggled, Holly examined it closer. It had dried out now and its glow was fading like the last embers of a beach fire. Soon it just resembled another piece of wave-polished sea glass.

So, after the briefest of debates, with a collective shrug they popped it into the blood-red bucket and set off again looking for the real treasure, which somehow seemed to elude them for another season.

Later, sensing their disappointment despite the usual excited chatter as they trudged back, Nanna Jo met them at the door with a smile as broad as the beach and a tray of freshly baked shortbread that they could smell halfway home.

"So," she twinkled, "what pirate booty have you brought for me this time?"

She had then reached into the bucket, sifted through the flotsam and pulled out the stone, which had now taken on the hue of Cornish clotted cream.

"Well, look at this. It will be just perfect. Just the right size," she smiled to Pop, a knowing grin on her face.

He looked up over the top of his glasses, put down

his book and made for the glue in the half-stuck kitchen drawer.

While the girls washed the shortbread down with fresh strawberry smoothies, Dad got the rickety stepladder and fixed the stone in place at the top of the arch.

"I am going to call it the Moonstone," announced Holly, "because it looks like something Tim Peake would have brought back from space."

Being fans of the UK's famous astronaut, the girls nodded their agreement then headed back to their families with tall tales to tell.

The little cottage then settled back into its gentle holiday rhythm.

Later that night, however, a particularly humid and light night, the first of the stories stole into the girls' room and danced wildly upon Holly's dreams.

Storms broke across the shoreline of Holly's consciousness while she struggled for deep sleep in the witching hours nearly a year ago.

Brightly coloured visions of fantastical creatures burst into her mind like the giant waves that crash over the harbour walls and threaten to drown the famous church tower.

Fantastical images swam into and out of focus in her dreams. Shiny tails, fancily-clad folk, horns, wings and hooves flashed past the horizon of her mind, tossed in waves like a herd of wild white horses, frothing, foaming and crying out a sound, a word, a name… her name.

And all the while the roars of the bullying wind failed to drown out the sweet sound of organ music, like a crazy fairground carousel.

When she surfaced back in the real world she had been calling out, "Those animals! Those creatures," arms flailing wildly.

She only calmed down when she realised she had escaped the clutches of the dream and was actually safe once more in her father's arms.

"Wake up, darling," she remembered him mouthing softly. "Wake up. You're having a bad dream."

And when she managed to focus her eyes, she saw

Lucy over her Daddy's shoulder, her eyes as wide as saucers, pointing.

"Holly," she mouthed… "you're on fire."

When Holly and Dad looked up, startled, her bed and her wall were alive with flickering orange and golden lights. For the briefest of seconds, the bedroom lit up like Christmas night.

Then, just as suddenly, before she could reach out to touch the fireworks, they went out, disappeared.

"What was…?" mouthed Holly.

"I have absolutely no idea," her father replied, an unusually worried look on his ever-calm face.

"I know!" Lucy said, jumping out of bed and taking down a large, battered book from the top of the chest of drawers.

Recognising it instantly, having spent many a sleepy hour in its company lulling the ladies off to sleep, Dad simply smiled indulgently.

"I'm not sure the Ashridge Forest fairies have found us down here yet, darling. It's a long way for little wings to fly from Hertfordshire."

Lucy wrinkled her brow and frowned with determination, leafing through the big book, searching.

Meanwhile, Pop kissed his youngest on the top of her head and tucked her back in with the book before heading to the kitchen with Holly, who seemed much better now, to warm up two mugs of chocolate milk.

Predictably, Lucy had fallen fast asleep by the time they returned to the pastel bedroom. So he sat on the old green chair and sang gently to his eldest daughter.

She smiled and gradually drifted off as her breathing became heavier and deeper. The soothing drink and soft song were working their magic.

On his way out, just before reaching for the crescent moon nightlight, he bent down to pick up the *Book of Fantastical Faerie Folk*. It must have slumped to the carpet when Lucy sank back into the land of nod.

As he went to put it back in its usual place, he was momentarily drawn to the last page she had been looking at.

It was a story about a Cornish mermaid. But strangely it was not a story he could recall reading to them before.

It was beautifully told and artfully drawn.

As his imagination folded into the evocative tale, there, in the skilfully crafted picture of a Cornish scarlet sunset breaking through a malevolent storm, he was greeted by the sight of a young girl at sea.

His mouth opened slowly as the realisation dawned that it was a very familiar face staring back at him, smiling.

Whether the sudden decision to leave early the very next day had anything to do with the odd events of that night, the girls never really discovered. But the adults were already packing to leave for the long drive back to the Shires when they awoke in the morning.

Of course, both sisters asked a hundred times why their holiday had been cut short so suddenly.

They even tried to drag their feet by insisting that they visit each of their friends before leaving, making them late taking to the road.

But their father wouldn't say why they left early. He simply blamed the weather as they raced the gathering storm clouds all the way back up the motorway evading the forecast full blue, magical harvest moon.

That was last year, and for two girls doing so much growing up so fast it seemed like an age ago.

This year's Summer Treasure Hunt Saturday blew in early from the west. For the first time in living memory, it was a windy midsummer's day, the clouds moody and brooding and quite a difference from the blazing sun just a year before.

The group of friends gathered on the shoreline in brightly coloured macs and wellies, some bought en route.

Elizabeth's corner shop received an unexpected boom in trade that morning as Cornwall's famous weather showed unseasonal teeth. But the treasure hunters were not going to be put off by a mere blowy spell.

Jack, the latest addition to their little gang, joined them, which put a smile on everyone's faces. He was their master digger and wasn't bothered by the weather; his ragged fawn and white coat saw to that.

"Come on, JJ," said Holly, slapping her legs as she ran down the beach with her sister and friends.

When the leaf-coloured National Trust officer blew the whistle and started the annual scramble for precious things with more of a windy grimace than a smile, Jack shot off ahead, barking excitedly as he sprinted past the competing families and casual crews. He disappeared round the headland, kicking up sand as he ran, oblivious to the cries of the girls, which were drowned out by the howling of the wind and the crashing of the wild white horse waves.

The juvenile posse gave joyous chase, of course, passing the usual treasure-hunting grounds on the way to the pools at the water's edge.

They wouldn't get much time to search this far out, given that the tide would turn in under the hour and start to submerge the beach and rock pools alike.

Holly had set her purple watch alarm to the tide time, one of the many important lessons her father drummed into her down the years.

As they arrived at the pools, Jack was barking excitedly and digging like a thing possessed.

Niamh and Reanna went to help him. But after ten minutes of digging they only pulled up some sort of smelly rag. They left the excited terrier to play as he rolled and wriggled himself all over it, as doggies do.

"Ewww," they all cried.

"Why do dogs have to do that? It's gross," said Reanna.

"My mum says it's to cover up their smell when they hunt for rabbits," said Alex.

"Cover it? It makes it worse. The rabbits will smell them coming from miles away," said Niamh.

"Unless the plan is to smell like a fishy thing, of course," said Holly. "That must confuse a poor bunny," she laughed.

"That's put me right off my pasty," Lucy moaned, as she placed their picnic rucksack by one of the larger rocks.

"Well, let's get hunting ourselves," said Holly eagerly, ruffling Jack's head and making for the biggest pool in an outcrop of granite rocks.

The girls split up to cover the most ground.

Early finds were quite encouraging as they unearthed a trove of shiny things.

Along with several pieces of smooth sea glass, they found a couple of colourful, sparkly spinners left by the fishermen and handfuls of unicorn shells.

Lucy came across a 20p piece in a green bottle and Niamh found a very pretty broken locket in a rock pool, rusted shut, of course. But they didn't have much luck finding the sort of treasure hidden as part of the competition, like bags of golden coins, medals, pretend jewels and such.

When the returning water started to creep up on them, erasing their footprints as it selfishly took back the beach, they decided to call it a day.

Alex had grazed her knee quite badly in her clamber over the barnacle-encrusted rocks. It had been numbed by the cold but was starting to smart a bit now. The makeshift bandage they had made out of a picnic serviette kept blowing off and she needed a plaster, really.

The girls gathered their things and retreated to just above the high-tide line. They stopped briefly to munch on their pasties, eat the fresh juicy apricots and drink the cherry pop Nanna Jo had slipped into their picnic lunch.

While they were eating, Holly realised that Jack had wandered off again.

"Alex needs to get back. You three go with her. I'll find him and then come and join you at the Fat Mackerel," she suggested.

"But Dad said we shouldn't leave anyone on their own," protested her sister.

"I'm not, silly. JJ is with me," Holly smiled.

Knowing how headstrong their friend could be and comforted by the fact that this was virtually their home village, at least in the summer, the friends reluctantly left Holly.

After hugs they set off across the sand, carrying their bucket of booty with them. The way back always seemed longer than before, much like car journeys home do.

Holly waved them off, then packed up the picnic and went looking for the naughty furry boy. It was starting to drizzle a little now. The wet wind felt clammy on her face and she could taste the sea spray at the corner of her mouth.

She didn't have to go that far to find their terrier.

Predictably stubborn and determined, he had returned to the spot on the other side of the rocks where he found the smelly rag earlier.

He was now growling while he tugged at something poking out of the sand, shaking his head vigorously with the cloth in his mouth.

Holly laughed to herself and jogged over to her little ragged dog. But the smile quickly turned upside down when she got there.

Jack's filthy rag was still lying abandoned in the sand where Niamh had left it, the cold water now licking at the dry material, about to drag it back out to sea.

Jack's attention was instead focused on something different, something new. And, judging by what Holly could already see of it, it was something very special indeed.

Holly could tell from the red velvet material she could see already that what Jack had somehow found had belonged to someone very important.

What it was doing here on their beach she didn't know. But the more they uncovered as they scrabbled with palms and paws, the faster the mystery grew.

Strangely, the material wasn't dirty or smelly as you would expect from something that had been on the beach for, well, who knows how long? It was a bit moist in parts. But it wasn't soiled or stained, not even after JJ's persistent attentions.

After about five minutes of digging, she could tell that it wasn't a dress or a coat as she had first thought. It seemed to be something people hardly ever wear apart from on stage or when dressing up. It was a robe or cloak. And where it fastened at the front she could now make out the letter E in very fancy, untarnished gold metal.

Encouraged by the fact that it seemed pretty clean, and oddly not that damp, Holly gave it a good shake and then slipped it around her shoulders.

This seemed to amuse Jack a great deal and he ran around her in excited circles, barking like a cheering crowd.

Holly turned to face the wind and the cape unfurled

behind her with a snap, like a very fancy ship's sail, flicking off grains of sand as it did. It was a perfect height and size for her and made her feel very grand indeed.

Picking up a long driftwood stick, she playfully pretended to hold court while the terrier jumped and gambolled about her. "Arise, Sir Jack," she laughed as he now bit into the end of her gnarly staff.

Distracted by their find and perhaps a little fooled by her fantasy thoughts, quite out of character, Holly had failed to keep an eye on the creeping water and must have inadvertently turned off her alarm. Then she noticed that her feet were splashing wet.

The sun had dipped down behind the headland hill and, as the twilight ebbed in, she could see that the sea had already cut them off from the main beach.

Stuffing the new find into the space created by their brief feast, Holly quickly fastened the rucksack with numb fingers and slipped it over her shoulders.

Driftwood staff in one hand she scooped an ever-wriggly Jack up into the other. The water was already up to his tummy.

Lucky she was wearing wellies, she thought, as she turned to head back in the direction the others had gone.

It was then that she clearly heard the first loud splash.

S plashing is a funny thing.

Sailors often report that a splash can be heard even during the worst of storms. Somehow our sensitive senses are tuned to the signs of distress and Holly's senses, famously more sensitive than most, were crying out that something was wrong.

She ran to the source of the sound, which was just the other side of the last green and grey rock that was rapidly disappearing beneath the returning sea.

Jack and long stick still in hand, she expertly leaped from rock to rock until she reached the top and could see through the swirling surf.

The sleet was almost a watery sheet now, whipped up by the growing wind that stung her face like a flicky damp towel.

She scanned the water for signs of life, half expecting, half hoping to see one of the seals that visited this beach from time to time, forgetting again the danger they were in.

But there was nothing in the water and, as Jack's barks reminded her, they really had to go.

He wriggled free and dropped to a patch of damp sand on the rocks. As she stooped to pick him up again, she heard it once more, an unmistakable splash, but this time she thought she heard an accompanying cry.

"Help me."

Without a second thought, Holly jumped the three feet into the shallower surf. The cold sea water instantly filled her boots but this was forgotten when Holly spotted the girl being swept towards the rocks.

Jack was barking uncontrollably now as wave after wave crashed near them, sending cold spray in arcs.

Holly knew she had to act quickly before she had two rescues on her hands and, leaning on the driftwood staff, she reached out and grabbed the girl by her outstretched hand.

"Use your legs to push towards me," she mouthed above nature's noise.

Then, somehow, she found the strength to pull them both onto what was left of the shoreline, heaving and gasping as they collapsed in a sodden heap.

Moments later they were joined by a very soggy terrier as Jack made his own way to them, half paddling and half belly-surfing as only he knew how.

He was the first to greet the stranger properly as he darted up her chest and started licking the salt water from her face without waiting to be invited.

"Jack, get off!" said Holly. "What happened? Are you ok?" she asked, finding it hard to conceal the concern in her voice.

The stranger, however, gingerly swept her wet blonde hair from her face and simply smiled.

And, when she eventually opened her mouth to speak, Holly could hear nothing but the sounds of the sea.

What happened next was a blur for a long time. When Holly first woke up in her bed at the cottage, the dreams had taken over again.

She remembered Pops by her bedside, holding her hand, Nanna wiping her brow gently or kissing her face.

But in between, all she could recall were the dreams.

In her delirium she was often sort of flying, floating just above the outstretched hands of twisted creatures clutching at her, faces contorted, dribbling mouths agape.

Others had huge fangs and claws that they clacked together like huge scissors, snipping and slashing obscenely.

Eventually, from the shadows burst four figures clad in light, chastising and then chasing the wicked ones back to their lairs only for them to catch fire, regroup and hunt her, again and again.

It took a day for the fever to break and, when Holly finally came round, the first thing she noticed was the velvet cape draped over the bottom of the patchwork quilt on her bed.

So it hadn't all been a dream.

Dad was asleep on the green chair. He had obviously been there all night, perhaps a few nights, and even in his sleep looked exhausted.

Lucy was flat out in her twin bed on the other side of their room, snoring sweetly.

Holly slipped from beneath the sheet, not wanting to disturb her family, and, despite shaky legs, avoided the creaky floorboard as she crept from the room.

She was very thirsty and poured herself a long glass of elderflower cordial from the jug in the pantry.

She then nestled down in the cushions on the window seat that the light always visited first, after it danced over the harbour water.

She yawned and sighed. It was a lovely dawn, quite the loveliest she could remember since, well, since they had been coming to this coast.

As her turquoise eyes lazily watched the seabirds head out to their favoured fishing spots, she sleepily but gradually recalled the events on the beach.

And then she remembered the girl.

"Where is she?" she thought, in part panic. "What happened? How did I get back here?"

Then she noticed that the dawn sunlight was glowing particularly warmly at the front of the house. Their white gate flashed almost orange in the rays reflected from the wall on which the mystical archway stood proud.

Holly got to her feet, drawn by the light, Nanna's shawl falling to the floor as she crossed to the door.

Then she slowly reached for the large black key. But

her heart skipped a beat when she realised that the door was already unlocked.

As she gently pushed the top half of the door slowly open, she could tell that something was different; something important had changed.

There, sitting on their shell-mosaic and iron bench, was the blonde-haired girl she had rescued from the waves. Above her, iridescent and pulsing like a gentle heartbeat, was their Moonstone.

Was it humming ever so very quietly?

The mysterious Moonstone was alive. Yes, alive, and radiating the gold and silver twinkling light that they had thrilled at last summer when it danced on their bedroom wall.

Holly's gaze was torn between the beautiful light show and the girl. She felt a strange mixture of awe and wonder and a tinge of what must have been fear, as she sensed at that moment that everything in their lives was about to change.

"Hello!" said Holly, placing her hand gently on the pale shoulder of their visitor as if to check that she was real and not an overspill from her delirious dreams.

The girl turned her head, not in surprise as you would imagine, but with a warm welcoming smile, as if she was expecting her to be there.

A slender hand made a gesture with her mouth until Holly realised that the girl, who looked just a little younger than her, couldn't speak.

"Don't worry," said Holly, "I have an idea." She disappeared back into the cottage for a minute or two before returning with a pad and the bright coloured pencils they used for drawing.

"We can use these."

Just then the Moonstone pulsed again and Holly looked up to see a kaleidoscope of colours dancing on its milky face.

"I've never seen anything like the way it's reflecting the light this morning," said Holly. "Have you?" But to her great surprise the girl nodded.

When Holly looked down at the paper, she was astounded to see a beautiful drawing of her stone, but not as a stone on its own; it was now part of a necklace containing what looked like seahorses, dolphins and pretty fish.

"You've seen this stone before?" Holly whispered. The girl nodded, then picked up the pad again and started to write. This time, it was a name: Savannah!

Then she pointed to herself and smiled at Holly again.

"It's lovely to meet you, Savannah," Holly said, with a relieved voice. "I was so worried about you when you were in the water. I thought that you had... you had..."

And then, quite unexpectedly, she started to cry.

Her new friend put her arm around Holly until she had composed herself again.

"There's so much we need to talk about, to understand together. Yet somehow I feel like I've known you all of my life."

And there the two girls sat together, gazing out across the waking harbour, an early morning sight usually reserved for just the fisherfolk and the birds.

Holly didn't know whether it was the first tentative rays of the morning sun, but she felt warm and secure next to her blonde-haired companion.

So there they stayed for quite some time until the rest of the residents of their little cottage gradually started to stir.

"Morning, ladies," yawned a sleepy-eyed Pops as he staggered out barefooted and sat down on the wall.

"What a glorious day it promises to be, and how happy I am that we're all safe and sound and back here together. You gave us quite a scare," he said, looking lovingly into Holly's eyes. "If it hadn't been for Savannah here coming to fetch me, I shudder to think what could have happened."

Holly felt the surprise rise in her tummy but forced it back down again with a shrug and a smile. Something told her that there was more to this than she understood now, so she simply reached out and held her father's big hand.

"I'm sorry, Daddy," she said sheepishly. "You know how crazy JJ can get and…"

Taking his cue, the terrier sprang into life where he had been snoozing and started licking the sides of her mouth, making her giggle and gag.

"We're all just relieved that you're ok now. Savannah wanted to stay with you until you recovered from the fever and we're grateful for the way she helped look after you."

Savannah started writing on the pad again, suggesting

that she would have to go this morning as she was expected elsewhere.

After she and Holly arranged to meet up again later in the week, they said their farewells and set off along the harbour road. She was last seen making her way down the harbour steps to the beach.

"Lovely girl. Does she live round by Kynance Cove?" asked Pops. "I must say I've not seen her and you never mentioned her before."

Holly didn't answer because, of course, she couldn't, given JJ's constant attention. So when he finally jumped off her lap at the smell of bacon frying, she smiled again and pretended to drift back off for a nap, her face lit up by the morning sun.

She loved a mystery and what a delight that this one was, right here, right now in her favourite time and place.

Just then Nanna Jo popped her head round the door. "How's our little mermaid?" she asked, that cheeky grin all over her face. "Gave us all quite the scare, you did. Quite the scare indeed."

"Oh, I'm fine, Nanna," Holly replied. "Just need to listen to Pops more and actually use the tide alarm," she laughed.

"Of course you're alright. You always are. I meant our new friend. How's she? And where did she come from? It's not every day that time and tide bring someone so special to our shores.

"Yet, judging by the way the Moonstone has been behaving since your dad carried you back last night, this friend is someone special."

And, as if on cue, in response to the warming caresses of the morning sun as it peeped out from behind a fluffy cloud, the archway burst into a light display that would have dazzled any lighthouse keeper.

Little did the adults suspect, but things were about to change for Holly and her loved ones.

Yet not even such a clever girl as Holly could ever imagine how much and how fast.

Down at The Fat Mackerel Cafe, excitement crackled and bubbled over onto the pavement, enticing passersby to step inside.

Whacky Sally-Anne, the purple-haired owner, had "magic at her fingertips", Pops always said. Her sausage sandwiches were the stuff of legend and the atmosphere she created with her wild paintings, crystals and chimes warmed the heart of even the most cynical blow-in or townie.

"One more milkshake, ladies?" she enquired, waving the stainless-steel mixing jug above her head and moving her sensual hips and flowing skirts to the world music on the sound system.

They nodded in enthusiastic chorus and then swooped back down to the object in focus: a note; a note from the enigmatic Savannah, immediately obvious from her wavy, eccentric writing.

Dearest Holly.

I am so grateful to you for everything you did for me when we met.

You don't know just how much peril I was in when you found me. I'm also so very pleased that you haven't told the grown-ups the whole story yet, as they seldom understand.

I'm sure you have so many questions to ask.

Can you come and meet me, at low tide, by the rocks where you found me and I'll try to explain as best I can?

Your very special friend
Savannah

"What does she mean?" cried Niamh.

"Can we all go, Holly?" Alex blurted. "I would so love to meet her too."

"Please, Holly," she implored, spilling a bit of her refilled shake in her urgency to grasp her friend's hand and squeeze tight.

"I don't think it's a good idea," said Lucy, once again acting older than her years. "Savannah doesn't really know any of us. There is clearly something secret going on. I don't want to get into trouble. And, anyway, if we're ever going to solve the mystery, it's best that Holly goes alone."

She was clearly trying hard to cover up the fact that she was a little jealous about her sister's new friend, but failing.

So, despite the cries of the gang and leaving Jack straining at his leash in the care of the crew, Holly set off at midday.

She was soon back at the site of the events of that dramatic Saturday.

Just for fun, she had brought the scarlet robe with her, hidden in a carrier bag. She pulled it about her as she sat down on the flattest rock to wait, being sure to tuck the bag away in her pocket.

She wasn't there for long before the figure of her friend appeared from the seaward side of the beach, looking radiant in a long ocean blue dress and golden hair band. She smiled as she saw Holly, who stood up to greet her.

"Don't you find that this is always a little bit of a blowy spot?" Holly said, forgetting for a moment that Savannah had no spoken words.

Savannah smiled, looked deep into Holly's eyes and then took her hand and led her towards the cliff face.

It looked as though they were headed for a dead end, but it must have been an optical illusion caused by the way the boulders were lying. Soon, much to Holly's surprise, they were at a part of the beach that she hadn't noticed was accessible before.

Here, their footprints seemed to be the very first, not just for this tide, but ever.

After a short walk, they approached what looked like a solid rock wall, covered in ivy and seagrass.

Savannah reached forward and drew the grassy and leafy covering aside like living curtains. She then gestured for Holly to follow her inside.

What greeted them as they stepped, blinking, into a cool, cavernous, salty-smelling space simply took Holly's breath away.

The echoing cave was more fresh than cold and the silvery walls sparkled with a light from a source that wasn't obvious to the naked eye.

It was much bigger than Holly was expecting and could have been disconcerting had it not been for her companion's reassuring presence.

But the biggest surprise of all she saved until last when she turned to Holly and spoke – yes, spoke – with a voice as soft as a summer breeze.

"Welcome to my home, sister. I've been searching for you all of my life."

It was Holly's turn to be dumbstruck as her slight companion gently led her to a large rock wall, down which a constant flow of water cascaded.

With a wave of her hand, the water parted to reveal a series of pretty drawings, etched into the stone. And there, right in the middle, was a dark-haired figure in a scarlet cape standing by a pool of water in which a mermaid swam.

When Holly turned to see Savannah's reaction to her own, her friend had gone and was now swimming around the crystal water towards the back of the cave, water that gave off a very gentle light blue light.

"I'm sure this is all a great shock to you, Holly. But

I hope you understand that I had to bring you here. It is only here that I can be my true self and only here that I can give voice to the answers I know you will want to hear."

At this she glided effortlessly onto a smooth rock platform with one light flick of her beautiful jade-coloured tail. An actual, real, shiny tail.

"Are you ready, my sister, my friend?"

Holly's own legs threatened to give way beneath her and she thought she was fainting again for a brief second. This place seemed to buzz with a sort of friendly power that filled every part of her. So she sat down upon the soft sand and nodded eagerly to her friend, both excited and nervous about what the next few minutes would bring.

"I call this the Legend of the Lost," she said, gesturing towards the captivating picture sequence. "I am sorry that I do not know the whole story, but I have spent as long as I can remember swimming the wide oceans tracking down what I can about the family I have been cruelly separated from for many years.

"This has been my home for some time now and I have gathered what I know about our people here. It is our record, our legend, our legacy. Our story, if you will."

She pointed to the waterfall wall as she talked. "I have had to piece together the flotsam and jetsam from tales from various sources, from the legends and myths of fisherfolk to the stories the sea creatures sometimes share."

Holly, bursting with excitement, just smiled encouragingly, not wanting to interrupt her flow.

"It seems that some years ago, when you and I were little more than toddling babes, we may have been on a ship sailing from our home land with our family.

"It was a trip our parents were reluctant to take, but they were forced onto the sea by people who clearly meant us harm.

"Something perilous happened during that infamous journey that made the seabed bubble and bleed with fire and the oceans rise up like tall mountains.

"Many sea creatures were taken ill and died and many people were swept away by the sea's fury that winter.

"As the legend has it, the oceans were hell-bent on revenge against people who had forgotten to treat all life with respect and were abusing it by pillaging the oceans and ruining the land.

"Some sort of ancient sea crone stirred up the villagers where we lived and somehow our family was blamed for the anger of the oceans.

"We tried to flee but instead, as a sacrifice, an offering to calm the anger of the seas, we were captured and placed aboard a leaking ship called the *Romany Soul*, then cruelly cast adrift.

"I don't know what happened aboard that ship on our fated journey, but, from what I've learned so far, you and I may be the only survivors of that magical storm."

"But how can that be?" said Holly, clearly stunned by what she had just heard and full of questions. "The sea does get rough here but nothing like that," she cried.

"We don't live here all the time but, when we do, the local people are always fine with us. There hasn't been a big storm like that here. I have my family and you... you're..."

"A mermaid?" Savannah replied, smiling knowingly, as if she had expected a reaction like this from the confused girl. "Well, I usually lose my mermaid powers if I don't bathe in this pool for long enough or if I try to leave the cave or ocean when the moon is not exactly right.

"That's how you found me.

"I was drawn from the pool by the pull of the Moonstone, which had been lost but which you found.

"You've seen how it shines when on dry land. I went searching and didn't get back in time. It nearly killed me."

Holly nodded, frowning slightly. "I understand what you're saying. But surely, if there's any truth in what you've just told me, that would mean that I... I mean that I have..."

"Mermaid powers too?" asked Savannah, expecting that question.

But, before she could finish the sentence, Holly had taken off the cape and dived, head first, fully clothed, into the radiant blue water.

Savannah waited patiently for Holly to surface, which took a little less time than she anticipated.

The cold water had clearly come as quite a shock to her system and, despite being a strong swimmer anyway, Holly was gasping and spluttering when she bobbed back up.

"Ooohhhh, I don't know how you do it," Holly shouted through chattering teeth. "It's f–f–f–freezing."

She quickly gripped an overhanging stalactite, although with some difficulty, and scrambled out of the water with considerably less finesse than her companion had done.

Savannah raised an eyebrow and nodded down to Holly's lower body. There two very leg-like legs still stood proud but covered in goosebumps now and certainly not beautiful, iridescent shiny scales.

Holly wrapped the cloak round her with shivering hands and instantly felt better, like during a warm hug from a loving friend.

"Well, I guess that settles one of the questions we both had," said Holly, finding it hard to disguise the disappointment tinged with relief in her voice.

"But I was so sure," Savannah replied. "Everything about you is so right. You have the stone, the cloak; we even look and think alike. And when you were sleeping, I could feel your unsettled dreams as I have those dreams too."

"There are a lot of things that are hard to explain, lots of similarities," Holly replied.

"But lots of things that don't, too. What about the colour of our hair? I'm dark yet you're blonde? What about our eyes? Mine are blue and yours green. I already have a family. Then there's the fact that I found those objects on this beach, not to mention a certain deficiency in the tail department."

At that they both laughed out loud.

"I actually can't believe this is happening," said Holly, wrapping the robe more tightly around her again to warm up.

She was surprised to notice that her teeth chattering stopped as suddenly as it started once its warmth caressed her shoulders.

"Tell me more of what you've found out so far and this time I promise to stay on dry land."

"Well, I've been here as long as I can remember," Savannah replied, in a wistful tone.

"In that time I've saved dozens of people lost at sea, without them realising.

"A couple of years ago I rescued a sailor from a shipwreck off Lizard Point, a few miles from here, where he had been fishing.

"He was very old and a bit delirious, mumbling about witches and sea cats and serpents and such.

"But while he was recovering he told me how he

knew someone who knew someone who knew the legend of our fated boat ride in the storm, way back when. He even sang part of an ancient mariner's sea shanty, apparently written about us.

"He was the one who described the scene you see before you on the wall. He was adamant that, as the old story goes, at least some of us survived the waves.

"Based on what he told me and other clues I've gathered, I am certain that our parents and the rest of our family are still very much alive."

"Alive and living here in England?" asked Holly.

"Well, yes, I think so. But what happened to us wiped my memory, like the tide picks the sand clean every night.

"Whenever I change from one form to another, it seems to set my memory back a bit too, at least for a while.

"Recollections only really come to me like driftwood drawn by the ebbing and flowing of the tides and current.

"But every time a new piece falls into place I update it in here, on this wall, as you see."

Holly examined the drawings a little more closely and, as expected, she could see two adults, representing Savannah's parents, and four children, two blonde, one dark-haired and one with red hair, all holding hands.

Some sort of black bird was depicted in a tree above them, wild animals cavorted in fields and in the distance dark, smoky clouds and large waves loomed.

The strange scene made her feel sad for a moment.

"How would I feel if I didn't have my own little

family?" she thought to herself. "What would I do if I were all alone, stuck between two worlds, like my new-found friend?"

It was these overwhelming emotions that made Holly commit to the second large leap of the day as she turned to Savannah and said, "My head is spinning with all of this and I don't know what to think about what you've just said. But I promise you that I will do everything I can to help you with your quest. I really can't imagine what it would be like to lose my family as you have. I can't just turn away.

"I know you can't be far from this special place for too long.

"But please come and join us at the cottage for a while. I know Dad and NJ will be delighted to see you again. Lucy is desperate to know you and our friends can't stop talking about you.

"That way you and I could at least do some planning about how to get to the bottom of your story."

Savannah smiled indulgently as if she was expecting Holly's response and after considering the implications of Holly's request, replied.

"I can stay on dry land a lot longer, it seems, when the conditions are right and when the full moon meets the Moonstone.

"The Moonstone clearly bestows greater powers on me than I have here, judging by our last adventure.

"I also seem to get power from being near you, Holly." She smiled as she spoke.

"Oh, that's great news. I have a very good feeling

about this," Holly replied, excited. "I really don't know why, but there has to be a reason I found this strange robe and the Moonstone."

"Let's go and work it out together if we can."

Then, with those optimistic words, the two girls readied themselves and arm in arm stepped back into the sunlight together, chatting excitedly about the adventures to come.

But as they walked back down the beach, heading to the harbour and home, neither of them noticed that someone or something, lurking in the long grass at the edge of the shoreline, had spotted them.

It tracked their progress around the point until they started to cross an area hidden from sight on the landward side.

Then, with a blood curdling scream, the first of the wild beasts broke cover, panting, slavering, eyes wild and howling like something terrible, in pain.

What happened next unfolded in what seemed like several minutes chastised by a horrified heartbeat but played back in freeze frame.

First, two sinewy animals, wolfish but running upright on horribly muscled legs, slammed into the back of the girls, forcing them apart.

When Holly landed she remembered seeing her companion rolling down the grassy bank holding fast to the manes of the beasts, riding one while clutching at the other.

But she then saw two more divert from the cliff edge from which the others had fallen.

Without having time to scream or even think, she was back up on her feet and sprinting, running for what now appeared to be her very life.

Holly gasped.

The sweat was flowing, running into her eyes, burning as she ran.

Lungs screamed, heavy, horribly dry.

She gulped down hot air, chest heaving with terror.

She could hear herself crying in panic –"Faster, run faster," – and she could feel the fine hairs, taut all over her body, prickling with fear.

She clawed through the mud and threw herself between the dark roots of an ancient tree.

Yet still the thud, thud, thud of the footsteps came.

They were relentless, like a pack of rabid horrors on the hunt.

And they were chasing her through the dark woods that everyone had told her to avoid at all costs.

But now it was too late.

She was on her own.

They were coming for her.

They were here…

At first she thought she had managed to confuse them as her fall had left her deep in the cradling fronds of a clump of ferns and tree roots.

But then she heard the distinctive noise of

something hound-like, sniffing at the air, filtering each tiny breeze for any trace of human scent.

Trembling, she pulled the red robe close about her as if it were her father's arms. Yet her blood froze as the hunched, dribbling abomination inched closer to where she was hiding, trying to stem her heavy breathing.

As the second vile creature joined its fanged companion, she could barely stifle a scream, so bit down hard on what she realised was the golden clasp of the cloak.

Just as she did this, both demon dogs snarled savagely and tore into the foliage where she lay.

But what happened next took everyone by complete surprise, not least our raven-haired reluctant warrior.

Holly suddenly experienced a sensation she later described as what she imagined spiders must feel when mistakenly sucked up the vacuum cleaner. She was somehow propelled backwards at a rapid rate of knots through blinding, rainbow-coloured light until, looking up, everything had changed.

The shade was ethereal and sparklingly brighter. She could see everything in bold colour. The plants were suddenly huge but somehow still in perfect proportion as they were before.

Everything was so much clearer, smelt rich and vibrant and fresh and, best of all, she was, yes, she was flying.

Holly noticed that her cloak had now gone and had transformed itself into a pair of translucent wings, like the tangerine gelatine from packet jelly.

The beasts were fast disappearing into the depths of the dark woods now, tails between their legs as if terrified of the glow her whole body seemed to be emitting.

Instead, from everywhere, flying creatures were emerging to join her; ladybirds, lacewings, fireflies and bumblebees, seemingly smiling as they teased and tumbled about.

"Hello, little ones!" Holly whispered in a relieved tone, but loudly. "Nothing to fear now; they've gone."

But then she remembered the last time she saw her companion and her thoughts changed from delight to dread in an instant.

As Holly reached the edge of the forest clearing, she seemed to find her feet instinctively and by the time she broke from the cover of the trees she was walking again, cape blowing in the stiff breeze.

She ran to the cliff side, then slowed tentatively as she reached the edge, half afraid of what she was likely to find.

Looking down, however, there was nothing but the wild water crashing on the hungry rocks below.

There were two dark, shaggy shapes in the water, which she took to be the monsters.

But there was no sign of Savannah at all, just a group of gulls crying hauntingly in vain at the last breath of a very long and incredibly traumatic day.

Book 2

The Willowand's Alive

Alice had never seen their hero like this before. Her blessing bow was broken and limp, she gripped her spear tightly, her face was soiled and her eyes were frozen with a wild fear.

"We must reinforce the shielding spell now.

They're upon us.

We've been betrayed.

Move…!"

Willow trees throb with an ancient magical power. Of all the trees that inhabit the forest, it is the tree most associated with water, the moon, the nature goddess and all that is feminine.

But, like many of nature's subjects, it also has a sinister, even malevolent side.

It has dangerous associations with tragedy, with mischief arising from tricky things not being quite as they appear.

The willow is the tree of dreaming, of intuition, of knowing things by instinct. It is the tree of deep emotions and magical sensations.

It can heal and it can harm. The powers of the willow are considerable, but, like many things about the forest, the willow is mostly mysterious and not fully understood.

Its powers are said to be at their greatest at the beginning of spring, when all life is stirring. For the willow often leads the way in rebirth, in giving life to new growth.

Is it any surprise, therefore, that so many magical artefacts are fashioned from the boughs of such powerful trees?

Or does it shock you to hear that it was in such an

ancient tree, by a deep, dark pond into which its emerald leaves were reflected like a mirror, that on one bright moonlit night a baby was found by the faerie folk, hidden in its boughs?

Deep in the forest was the second birthplace of this very special – some say magical – child.

There, by the glade, next to the twinkling, crystal pool, in the most magical and mystical of places, was where the special child was discovered, giggling as butterflies and ladybirds tickled its toes and its nose.

And it was deep in the darkest reaches of this forest that this special child was nurtured and taught the ways of nature by two households, and where it was destined to decide the fate of the child's entire family, a family the child never guessed they had.

Alice yawned and rubbed her eyes. The sweet birdsong that first caused her to stir was in full chorus, echoing gently around the glade.

She glanced over towards Henry, her brother and best friend, and could tell by the smile on his face and the faint mumbling noises and sudden jerky movements that hinted of sleepy adventure, that he was still dreaming.

Lifting the heavy, rainbow-patched eiderdown that was probably a bit much for this time of year, she did her best to slide out and into her raspberry fleece without waking anyone and slipped quietly outside.

It was a little damp where the mist met the dew on the lush green grass. But dawn was already starting to chase the last of the dark night over the hills that cradled them in their ample, pink bosom.

"It's so beautiful here," she thought to herself, as she did most days, except the drizzly ones, then she slipped on her yellow boots, chilly without socks, and headed for the glade.

There were to be no forest school lessons with Mother today. So she was hoping for a glimpse of badger cubs returning late to their sett amongst the tangled and crazed roots of the great oak, or perhaps surprise the young rabbit family nibbling the first dew-soaked growth for breakfast.

Alice picked her way carefully through the wild rose and bramble bushes, already alive with mini-bear-like bumbliebees.

She picked up a hazel switch and used it as a sword to slice a path through the abundant cow parsley and could smell the crushed wild garlic as she hopped over the trickling stream to where the gypsy strawberries grow.

Sometimes she would come across a deer and her fawn drinking the fresh hill water here. Neither ever seemed to notice her and she sat for what seemed like ages watching them, so comfortable together.

But not today. There seemed to be no furry friends about today. In fact, she thought suddenly, as she left the simple path and pushed through the long ferns, taking care not to disturb the abundant red-and orange-capped toadstools that sometimes exploded with powdery seed, even the wood pigeons had stopped calling now.

After another dozen steps, which she counted out in her head, the rich smell of lichen-infused damp leaf mulch competing for her attention, she arrived at what looked like a curtain of verdant, spear-shaped leaves. They were cool to the touch and almost seemed to shrink a little, shyly, when she moved to part them.

Alice didn't know what she was expecting as her eyes adjusted to the shade beneath the leaf canopy. But it certainly wasn't the sight of a tiny home and the brittlest, most beautiful creature she had ever seen, fast asleep inside, cosy on a bed of fresh, jade-coloured moss.

Wood nymphs are misunderstood.

True, some like to think they are the very definition of sweetness and light we see in the films. You know, all smiles and soft voices, glitter and sparkles and such?

But more often than not, they aren't like that at all, at least not all of the time.

In fact, some nymphs, like pixies or even goblins, but without the snot, of course, can be very, very mischievous indeed. They also have famous bad tempers if you get on the wrong side of them.

And they really don't like being woken up.

Somehow, Alice suspected it would be a bad idea to disturb this tiny creature. They had lived in these ancient woods all her life and she had learned that it is best to let sleeping things lie, both the normal and the mystical ones.

So she closed the leaf canopy carefully behind her and very, very carefully, retreated.

But now that her eyes had become accustomed to the light, she noticed that she seemed to be surrounded by a village of little houses. Since she noticed them, she also couldn't but notice that it wasn't shadowy in this part of the forest at all. In fact, there seemed to be a gentle light kissing the shade away. It was just the sort of light she was used to at home when she left her pretty string of nightlight candles on, as she did most nights.

It was fascinating to cast her eyes around the space.

There was a tiny bench made from what looked like bark and, yes, some pretty white mushrooms conveniently arranged around it. Or perhaps the mushrooms had been there first. She couldn't tell.

On one side of what looked like a tiny street was a rainbow-coloured cottage. She peeped inside and hanging from the thorns of a perfumed wild tea rose was the most beautiful buttercup-yellow little tunic with embroidered slits, which must have been for a delicate pair of wings.

A very handsome chest, encrusted with what looked like precious stones or jewels, glistened in the half-light, catching Alice's eye.

She knew she really shouldn't, but, like a jar of forbidden sweets, she was drawn to it and before she could draw another breath she had very carefully opened the lid.

To her surprise, there was a stick inside.

But, before she could make up her mind what to think, a voice like someone gently shaking a glass bell tinkled very clearly in her ears, as if someone her own size was speaking.

"Well, what do you think you're up to, young lady?"

And she knew at once that it was the previously sleeping nymph. She was presumably the owner of the house and the chest and now she was in trouble. So, faced with an impossibly embarrassing situation, Alice did the first thing that came into her mind and started to cry.

"I'm so sorry," she sobbed. "I didn't know anyone lived here, I've never been to this part of the forest and..." but she noticed that her mystical companion wasn't looking at her any more.

Her attention was captured and held by something at Alice's feet.

Alice's heart skipped more than one beat when she looked down and saw it. It looked like a brown snake, twisting and swelling beneath her. It was coming for her, scarlet mouth agape.

Then she screamed and she ran. Alice had run all the way back to their forest cabin and curled up in a ball on her patchwork quilt before the reality dawned about what she had actually just witnessed.

Of course, the kerfuffle she created trying to get back into the cabin in such a hurry had woken Henry and Mother up. But, after reassuring them both that she was fine, which given Mother's condition wasn't the easiest of jobs, they eventually settled back down to sleep.

Alice then lay there and stared at the patc hed holes in the wooden roof, images swirling through her mind and blurring into a whirl of glitter, laughter. "That voice," she thought, and "what on earth was that disturbingly sinuous snake doing in that lovely box?"

She couldn't throw off the feelings of nagging guilt

for having trespassed into that secret place uninvited. So she made a promise to herself that, this very evening, she would try to make her way back to apologise in person.

The rest of the day dragged its feet after she had made up her mind. All the usual chores that she normally tolerated out of necessity, like cleaning out the chickens and washing the pots or sweeping the porch seemed particularly painful today.

As a result, her brother was even less responsive than normal and spent most of the day reading while their poor mother sat sewing in her chair, singing quietly to herself, as she often did, even more distracted than normal.

"Why can't you concentrate, Alice?" she had said when she had burned the breakfast sausages. "You normally love cooking and now they're ruined," she complained. "It's like you've been during your lessons this week, head right up in the clouds rather than in your science books. You've not been yourself. Anything you want to talk about?"

But Alice simply smiled and made up for it all when she went out hedgerow-scrumping with Henry and they then made a delicious summer fruit crumble for dinner, bursting with early bramble berries and rhubarb.

She then started the singing, after dinner, with one of her own compositions, Henry's favourite, *The Tale*

of Creepy Creek, strumming her dark blue guitar and
wailing together:

> *That creepy creek*
> *it comes a creep a creep creep creeping*
> *to take away the weak fore sunrise*

They sang as their own sun set between the oak trees,
the leafy guardians who formed their cosy canopy.

Later, when the trio had downed the sticky dregs of
the last of their supply of cocoa and wild honeycomb,
Mother and Henry headed to their beds.

Alice, however, forced herself to stay awake, until
eventually even the final stubborn candle flickered and
sputtered, surrendering to the draw of the dark.

All cautious thoughts somehow disappeared then
and she slipped into the night once more and started to
pick her way through the trees and bushes by the light of
the moon and stars.

All around her, nocturnal creatures were sniffing
and snorting in their hunt for fruits and grubs.

A hundred little eyes reflected the moonlight in the
bushes and the bracken, like dim torches.

Strangely comforted rather than perturbed by the
noises, Alice worked her way, faultlessly, back to the
willow tree canopy in the glade that they had never
noticed before this morning.

She retraced her steps easily, as if it were a path she
had been drawn down many times before.

A strange green glow lit up the glade as the little girl approached as quietly as she could manage.

She could feel the thrilling sensation in her chest that comes from the promise of great fun, but with a tinge of something dangerous in store. It was that scary, dare, double dare sort of thing that grown-ups must somehow choose to bury deep inside or just let go of at some point.

Alice didn't have to wait for long for the fun to begin because, before she even reached the willow tree, she noticed that the curtain of leaves and branches had been parted, as if the tree itself were ushering her inside.

"About time," tinkled that crystal voice again. "You have some explaining to do, missy," she said. And there, at her feet, lay the snake, seemingly frozen solid.

As she got closer, Alice could see that the object, which was about two reasonably sized feet long, wasn't in fact a snake. It was a piece of wood, sort of a few thin branches wound around each other. She also noticed that, while everything beneath the willow canopy seemed to emit light, it was giving off a very definite, low, emerald glow.

"If you don't mind me saying, you don't seem very surprised to see me," said Alice, her voice coming over a little more fiercely than intended, a trait often commented on by her mother when she was caught doing something she shouldn't.

"What a strange thing to say," said the delicate little person, in a voice like crystal stars tinkling together in a hot summer's breeze. "But I've known you all your life, Alice."

And with that she reached down and offered her a tiny silver goblet and what looked like the tastiest honey biscuit she had ever seen.

"Remember these?" she asked, before taking a bite of her own and drinking from the vessel, encouraging Alice to do the same.

And when she did, to her surprise Alice found that she could drink and drink the sweet liquid nectar. It tasted a bit like peaches, plums and pineapple juice, but lots fresher, if you can imagine that.

The biscuit was also a lot larger in her mouth than out and, when it popped, it tasted of the most delicious nectar cream she could dream of.

It was only then that Alice realised that part of the reason why her nymph companion wasn't at all disturbed was that, somehow, they were now both exactly the same height, same shape and same size.

This came as quite a shock to her.

"Oh, here we go again," said her new, or perhaps not so new, friend, noticing the shocked look on Alice's face.

Alice had to sit down when Sylvane or Sylvie had finished explaining, as she had done countless times before, it seemed, that they were actually very good or the very best of friends.

They called her "the Changeling" because, for as many moon cycles as Sylvie could remember, her friend had appeared during the start of the crescent phase of the moon all empty-minded and confused.

She then grew increasingly more confident and learned during the gibbous phase: waxing with enthusiasm and power to half-moon and then bursting with faerie zeal during full.

But then the waning moon would come again as inevitably as the leaves colour and fall from the trees. So they would eventually have to start all over again when she reappeared, as she had done yesterday.

As the nymph (or sprite, as they are also known) explained all of this as patiently as she could, pointing to her few possessions, her pretty little room and her buttercup-coloured coat on the same peg she had seen the night before, the rest of the village started to drift over, beaming with fond greetings.

"Ah, merry new moon," smiled a rather chubby, ruddy-faced fellow, sporting wings that looked like they would struggle to keep him airborne for long.

"Oh, Nimbus," Alice surprised herself by saying. "I've missed you," she announced, hugging him as she spoke.

"Well, that's another improvement on last time," the dimply-cheeked chap announced.

"Yes, it took her a few hours to remember until you raided the cookies and jogged her memory," laughed a lithe and dashing wood nymph dressed in bottle green.

"Zephyr. Oh, Zeph, how are you?"

"Same as when you saw me yesterday," he teased, kissing her on the cheek as if it were the most natural thing in the world to do.

Soon the group had swelled to the size of a small, colourful cloud of cheeky chums who emerged from various impossibly cute dwellings to exchange glad greetings and tall tales of events in the glade since Alice's last visit.

You see, in spritish time, a human day is a very long time, very many days in fact, and although Alice had only been back in her human form for what seemed like a few hours, she had been missing quite some time from her rainbow house, with the daisy yellow door and the rose and daffodil furniture. In fact, this time she had been away for such a long time that the Willowand had started to wonder whether she was ever coming back.

The woodland nymphs of Ashridge Forest were so caught up in their chitter and chatter that no-one bothered to notice the animated collection of magical sticks and branches, rumoured to have a unicorn hair heart, that sulked by the door.

So the wand did what any self-respecting ancient artefact would do, were it capable of moving on its own. It morphed itself into a miniature green dragon and flew up to the seat of Zephyr's trousers while he was in mid-tale and, with one carefully directed steam breath, singed his buttocks at the point where they parted, until he started hopping on the spot.

"Aaahhhhhhh," he screamed, frantically patting his trouser area in an effort to end the hot stinging.

"Oh, Helygenn, I'm so sorry to have ignored you," said Alice, reaching across and tickling the tiny dragon under its chin until it settled on her arm, made its way to her tunic pocket and then returned to its original shape.

If it's possible for a bundle of sticks to smile smugly, that's what the wand was doing as it poked out, proudly.

"The wand seems to have missed you as much as we have," laughed Nimbus. "And as jealous as ever, I see."

But he quickly choked back the end of that laugh as Alice's pocket stirred and three or four purple stars bubbled out in more of a growl than a chuckle.

The Wood Nymph Council met that night in the quartz circle.

Firefly lamps lit the friendly throng, feasting on bowls of berry broth to keep their beacons blazing while the elders debated the important business of the day.

A particularly respected sprite, Helice as he was known, held everyone's attention as he described some especially troubling events on the fringes of the Ashridge Forest kingdom.

"Four fawns were taken in the last two moon cycles and it would appear that something has now started attacking the adults.

"Even a juvenile group of horned monarchs struggled to repel a small pack of berewolfs down near the Glahglade only two sundowns past."

"They seem to be growing bolder and more frantic," replied Zephyr.

"There were sometimes raids this far south, but on nothing like this scale. Could it be sign of the return to the solstice eruptions? There have been warnings on the winds for some time now, as we all know?" asked an aged nymph in bottle-blue tunic. "Our winged friends have been bringing news of fresh fire from the hills, we all know that.

"We're most likely safe under the ring shield. Yet many of our friends will be exposed."

"But surely evil power could not have returned to the Firehills? Not after all this time?" Sylvane asked their leader.

Clad in silver, Helice seemed to shimmer when he spoke. His was always a reassuring voice of measured calm.

Alice could sense the unease pass across the gathered band of mystical folk, however, and she could detect the strain behind the eyes of the elders. She may have had a particular talent for sensing the feelings of others, but she was pretty sure everyone else could feel the tension in the discussion too.

As several senior nymphs started to voice their concerns all at once, the chatter and rippling hubbub was rudely interrupted.

The sudden, unexpected arrival of one of the most respected of their kind, Dianah, the warrior who oversaw everything to do with safety and security, came as a shock.

She flew wildly into their midst, clearly out of control, and crashed into the crystal flames.

Alice had never seen their hero like this before. Her blessing bow was broken and limp, she gripped her spear tight, her face was soiled and her eyes were frozen with a wild fear.

"We must reinforce the shielding spell now.

"They're upon us.

"We've been betrayed.

"Move…!"

Before the panicking sprites could organise their scattering, the smell of the threat was upon them even before the monsters arrived. It was like the worst fox spray upon a festering carcass and it warned of much worse to come.

In the blink of an eye, huge snarling shapes crashed through the lower boughs of the trees, crushing the bluebell beds and bracken.

One of the visiting rainbow sprites had flown directly into the path of one of the sets of slavering jaws, terrified by the fiery orange eyes and rumbling growl. The beast opened its dribbling mouth mid-stride and snapped at the delicate ball of light. But it tasted nothing as the target disappeared in a precious puff of multicoloured stars.

Then Dianah deliberately flew in front of it to distract it from a group of infants huddled under a large leaf, and stabbed it in the muzzle; it chased her, howling, back into the dark wood.

At the edge of the glade, a row of pretty houses were destroyed in seconds as two of the creatures fought over what was, at first a family of emerald wood nymphs or silkies that somehow transformed into a pile of twigs. They tore and ripped at the wood in frustration.

Alice had flown up a hazel tree, pursued by one of the beasts, howling its intent. But she was shocked to see it use its front limbs and claws to climb almost as quickly as she could fly.

"These are no ordinary werebeasts," she thought to herself, thinking of the dog-like creatures of legend. She was deliberately inching out to the very tip of a long branch near the very top. When she got there, she turned to face her pursuer, smiling.

"Now who's a not very pretty boy, eh? Come on, there's a good, very bad puppy," she teased, holding her hand out as if to pat it.

Unable to resist, the monster gave a loud howl, snarled and began to nudge along the bough until, when within a foot or two of his tasty prey, the inevitable happened.

Alice smiled as she heard the branch first crack and then, as if the tree had done it deliberately, which, of course, it probably had, the branch gave way under the creature's weight. The monster fell as though shot and plummeted like a stone, leaving Alice hovering on her lace wings.

"Bye-bye, beastie," she waved sarcastically, as it fell then crashed onto the forest floor a long way down.

A quick glance around the glade revealed that, while her friends were clearly frustrating their attackers, their home had been overrun by foulness.

Sylvane and Nimbus were cunningly teasing and leading a pack of the creatures on a one way trip in the direction of the sinking swamp, where she imagined they would meet an unpleasant end.

Helice and Zephyr had formed a protective diamond with several of the other senior sprites and they had conjured a phantom whirlwind that mesmerised the monsters, giving the rest of the clan time to disappear or hide.

Yet there seemed to be an endless filthy stream of the foul creatures, who clearly followed one another's scent trail to their glade, a path laid down by those who had gone before.

"We are going to tire and our powers will start to weaken," Alice thought to herself.

But, just as hope gave a hint of fading, something nudged her fingers apart and into her hand.

She then found herself compelled towards the centre of the crystal circle by a force she couldn't actually see.

What happened next would be sung around campfires and remembered in tall stories for generations to come.

Onlookers remember it in different ways. Some recall Alice, Willowand in hand, eyes burning verdant green, chanting and morphing until she was the size and shape of a tree.

Others don't remember anything but the pulsing flash of light stemming from Alice herself. It was unlike any light they had ever seen before.

But what they all agree on was feeling the warming glow of good energy flowing into their bodies, a sensation some describe as the sense of love you associate with your closest and dearest when you are reunited after time apart.

This goodly glow rapidly rippled outwards until it filled the glade and then the meadow and then what must have been the entire forest.

It spread and pulsed with a steady rhythm, like a heartbeat, and then, when fully charged, suddenly erupted into a million lightning flashes of sharp emerald.

Each shard seemed to search out every dark and gloomy place and space, transforming any fear into overwhelming positive energy, a sort of nourishing hope against ill thoughts.

Then they were all gone. None of the violent, malignant beasts could survive, it seems; they simply melted into the soothing light.

Yet, where Alice had stood, the epicentre where the crystal forces met, there remained nothing but a beam of light reflecting an image, like a flickering cinema screen.

When the returning nymphs looked closer they could make out, in the beam, the projected image of the most azure-coloured, weeping willow tree, a face seemingly delicately etched into its mid-bark.

Then Zephyr looked down, searching for something with panicked eyes, and his heart sank as he saw the unmistakable shape of their very brave friend, slumped horribly like a damp pile of leaves on the mossy forest floor.

Back at the cabin on the other side of Ashridge Forest, Henry had woken with a start when he heard the howling.

He had tried to warn his mother of the black beasts before in his pictures. But all she did was warn him that he would have to go to see the pokey strangers in the town who used to talk about him using words like "special" and "different", but in a way that he knew didn't mean good. He didn't like those type of people. In fact, it seems, there were very few people he liked or trusted at all.

There it was again, he thought, his excellent hearing detecting another of the spine-tingling whines on the wind.

"Sounds like they are huntin' for somethin'," he muttered under his breath, his voice trembling a little with excitement as he peeped through the gap in the window shutters, the catch having broken long before he could recall.

Unable to see anything stirring in the dark, other than leaves rustling in the wind, Henry dropped his legs to the floor and tried not to tread on the creakiest of the floorboards as he made his way across their small hall to his mother's room.

Poking his head inside, he could see that she was in a deep sleep. She was also muttering something to herself, as she often did.

Confident that she wouldn't wake, he reached up and pulled his brown coat on, stepped into his smelly sandals and made his way onto their porch. He then sprang over the small flight of steps that would surely betray him.

Neither Alice nor Mum knew of his private trips across the meadow to his special teepee of bracken, bark and branches.

Nobody knew that Henry had a private place where he would go. Here he could be free from prying eyes and questioning tongues.

Nobody knew, that was, but the night-time friends who sometimes paid him a visit, if he was lucky and the air was still enough not to carry his scent on the breeze.

Tonight, Henry felt drawn to his secret place. His den of mysteries.

Something about tonight was very different. It was like waiting for a very special dinner cooking for too long in the oven while the aroma of the roasting drives you hungry mad.

The delicious night sounds were teasing, calling, drawing him outside.

So he hurried his step.

Despite the late hour and dark night, Henry seemed to have a sixth sense about his surroundings.

He could hear the littlest rustle.

He could see the vaguest outline of a shape.

He could feel their hearts beating.

So he never bumped into anything as he wound his way along the dark path to the deeper parts of the forest.

As the urgency gripped him in a tighter and tighter hold, he started to walk even faster.

Soon he realised that he had broken into a slight jog, which became a run and then a sort of lolloping gambol until he felt himself tingling all over and his forearms forced their way down and, yes, he was sprinting, free.

Yet he wasn't running like a boy any more. He was now galloping on all four limbs and eating up the fast rushing ground before him.

As his silhouette merged with the horizon he could see the midnight route ahead as clearly as if it was the middle of the day.

Then he threw back his head and howled out his exhilaration to the blushing moon and watching stars.

When Alice came round for the second time on that long day, she was greeted by Nimbus's round face, beaming as ever.

Many of her other friends were packed into the cottage drinking hot cups of sweet nectar tea and tending to their very many cuts and bruises. The werebeast attack had clearly taken its toll.

Outside, the fae villagers were working hard to restore the damage caused. The air was electric with friendly magic as wands were waved, houses rebuilt, shelters restored and delicate bodies healed.

Helice and Dianah were leading a security party, first sending out winged scouts to watch the outlying areas and forewarn them of any more evil activity.

Hummingbirds, moths, fruit bats and large black beetles flew off to do their duty at the leader's request. While at the edge of the glade, more magical folk were at work setting flare light traps and creating plunge pits and other devices to ensure that they weren't caught cold twice.

Helice and the elders had clearly combined their powers as the whole glade rippled with a purple haze of magical light. Alice knew this was the crystal shield spell, something the Nymph Council only used in times of grave danger.

There was a price to pay for the shield and she could see that crystals in the circle were fractionally darker than they had been the day before.

Eventually, if not replenished, they would lose all of their protective power.

"We can't live under the shield forever," announced Helice. "We are going to have to find a way to contact our strongest friends in the forest and to find out the extent of the troubles.

"It has been a long time since creatures like this have been brave enough to venture this far and we can be sure that, while they have had a shock, braver of their kind will eventually be back. They will not be able to resist the temptations here."

"Temptations?" asked Dianah.

"Yes. Us," he replied, with a grimace.

Alice had heard and seen enough and rose from the pretty pastel-coloured couch where she had been recovering. She felt sort of drained and bruised from the inside out, but other than that was relieved to see everything back in apparent working order.

Even Helygenn had returned to wand form and was lying still, for a change, in his nesting box on the rosewood table, never really far from her side.

At this point Helice and Zephyr appeared at the door. "Well, how's our Willowand warrior feeling?" their leader asked, a proud smile on his face. "I don't know how you did it and am, if truth be told, a little reluctant to enquire. But you certainly saved our skins there. We were about to be overrun as there were so many of them."

"It wasn't me… it…" she started to reply, but stopped half way, realising that she had no explanation either, other than it had something to do with the situation, her and, of course, her mysterious wand-creature.

"Always knew you were special," said Zephyr, with a twinkle in his pale blue eyes. "Now perhaps you can help us think of a way to make sense of what's happening, as it is very clear that a disturbing shift has taken place in the crystal power plane. Unless we can get to the root of it, what happened here is most likely only the start of troubling times to come."

That evening, after the hard work was done and the nymph village returned to its former modest glory, the elders met again in an emergency council.

Their debate ranged long past twilight and when it concluded it was obvious from the body language that whatever conclusion had been reached had difficult consequences.

So it was with mixed feelings that Alice and her closest friends responded to their leader's summons.

Unusually, Nimbus had the task of relaying the news, presumably because his bubbly manner would soften the blow of the decision.

"We have debated long and hard and, no matter how we look at the challenge, it seems that we are going to have to look beyond the glade for the help of a higher power.

"The shield will only last so long, so we need help with the problem at its source, the Fireills."

As he spoke, he was clearly troubled by the prospect and what he had to say next.

"We may be a resourceful folk, but we need help. Your Willowand created a vision of the help we need to source now. We need to reach out to the Prince of the Forest. We need the help and counsel of Hernunnos, the Greene Man."

Even the wisest and most experienced of nymph elders gave a sharp intake of breath at the mention of his name.

"As Nimbus has stated," said Dianah. "We need to break cover from here in order to have any hope of contacting him.

"He will be aware of the shift in the balance of our forest, but we need to go to him to prepare what is to come.

"I am going to take a small band of courageous rangers deeper into the forest to seek support. Zephyr and Sylvane, I ask that you fly by my side."

For a fleeting moment Alice felt her heart sink until Dianah turned to her and said, "Alice, we clearly need your leadership as well."

Inadvertently her head bowed, ever so slightly, and her chest swelled with pride.

It would appear that, finally, she had been accepted by the woodland nymph elders.

She didn't have time to worry about the dangers ahead, the uncertainties and the scale of the task. All she could think to herself was "I mustn't let them down" as she headed back to her little house to pack a few things for the journey, which wasn't easy, not knowing at all what to expect.

Yet, right on cue, she could swear that something yawned then stirred on the side table as if to suggest, in a voice that she may or may not have heard in her head, "Well, what more could you need?"

Mother had not been oblivious to the nocturnal wanderings of her children. Not oblivious at all.

In fact, she had secretly watched them coming and going from their cabin in this lost part of the forest since either was barely able to walk.

They were always so excited by their adventures that they never dreamed that she was watching them through supposedly tight eyelids.

And, like many children, they were so blinded by that innocence that affects most children, that notion that you are the first and only child ever to have grown smarter than the silly Olds, that you forget to notice that the adults really do see. Because, you see, they have most likely seen it all before.

For once, as hard as it may be to believe, they were special children too.

Alice had grown so used to the cloak of boring and preoccupied that Mother very deliberately wore that she had started forgetting she was there. And that is one of the sad parts of growing up, for parents and children too.

But, even if Alice had somehow bothered to watch her sleeping mother's eyes, there was something she would never be aware of. Because her mother had never shown this side to either of her children. It was known as the power of the all-seeing or the third eye.

Reaching to the back of the large fireplace, taking great care not to dip the frayed edges of her throw in the still-glowing embers, she found the hidden ledge and brought down a package wrapped in dark cloth.

Unwrapping it with well-practised hands, she revealed a small cast iron pot on legs. An ominous smile passed across her face as she took a flask from somewhere inside the folds of her covering, uncorked it and drank the contents.

She then crushed the glass flask into the bottom of the small cauldron, waited a few brief moments and then regurgitated the liquid from her stomach onto the glass, with a gasp. It instantly started to bubble and swell until a liquid with a quicksilver consistency filled the pot.

"Now, my little ones," she whispered in a cracked voice, the strain of the dark magic showing. "Let us see how you do the bidding of your destinies. Show me where the darkness spreads as this deliciously dire disease takes a tighter hold."

While she sat by the dying fire watching the story of the children's adventures playing out before her in the flickering depths of the cauldron, she too had forgotten to remain entirely alert.

Something was watching the watcher.

In the furthermost recess of the roof, in a gap between the thatch and a wooden beam, a lone wood nymph was taking in the strange scene.

What the good-spirited Nimbus saw troubled him. It troubled him more than he dared to think or could say.

For he had seen the wicked person in this scene before him before and, for Alice in particular, this was going to be very, very bad news indeed.

What the cauldron revealed was Henry, now transformed beyond recognition, in full lycan, weirwilde form, arriving at what looked like a carcass of something recently slain.

At first it looked like a very large creature, but it soon became apparent that it was a number of his kind feasting in the same set of shadows.

The others became agitated at his arrival and started snarling and winnowing, making a sort of "whoop, whoop" noise, baring their teeth and slouching their backs.

It was clear that he had some form of respect amid their kind and that what appeared to be a decent-sized pack were well acquainted with each other.

Just then the quicksilver mirror misted over and the scene shifted to one Nimbus knew well, the fern canopy on the fringes of their glade.

The crystal force field was clearly barring the dark magic from penetrating further, but the picture became clearer the more the small band of travellers moved from its centre.

Something between a smile and a sneer spread on the face of the werewytch as she watched. The modest band was clearly heading across the fertile meadow to the deepest and darkest recesses of the forest where few venture. This seemed to please her as she cackled quietly to herself.

"Fly, pretties, fly. Soon you will have spun a path to the very beating heart of the final destruction of that odious family.

"They shall never possess your power.

"It will pass back to the shades and a new age will begin at last."

Her cackling laugh froze Nimbus's blood.

He dreaded to think how this dark news would affect his very special friend.

The party of winged warriors made its way carefully through the long grass and wild flowers of the meadow, where handsome glis glis foraged, startling a gathering of snuffling hedgehogs on the way.

They were unable to fly across this open space for fear of attracting unwanted attention. As everyone knows, enchanted creatures always leave a following stream of light when they take to the air and they were desperate not to be tracked.

Perhaps you've seen these trails yourself, out of the corner of your eye, when you've been camping in the woods, or on a nature walk after dark with the grown-ups?

When they eventually made the fringe that led to the deepest part of the forest, the group paused to drink a little warming nectarmead wine and to nibble on raspberry sweetmeats.

"We need to keep our strength up," said Sylvane as she passed the provisions around.

You could always rely on Sylvie to look after everyone. She had the kindest of hearts and everyone loved her for it.

Predictably, Dianah paced while they snacked, ever keen to keep on the move.

She looked every inch the warrior in her scarlet tunic, owl helmet and boots. Her famous hawthorn spear was strapped to her back, with its needle-sharp tip and ability to fire blasts of concentrated, pure light.

Dianah may be tough. But she realised they had all been through an awful lot.

However, she had come face to face several times with the evil now facing them, didn't mind admitting that she was frightened and privately doubted whether they had the resources to see this battle out. For they were a peaceful, gentle folk at heart.

After a short while, however, her companions, as if sensing her unease, quietly slipped what they had left back into their small packs and they were soon on their way again.

Zephyr handed round the everlight torches he had been carrying.

They each snapped them to wake the finding fireflies inside, releasing a treacly feast for their companions in return.

"Show us the way, little friends," whispered Sylvane as, one by one, the companions followed the dark path into the gloomy artery that led to a place few of their kind had visited before and from where even fewer had returned to tell the tale.

Their route took them through a long avenue of dead pine trees that the forest creatures called the Hall of Sorrows. This was on account of the fact that so many alien species had been planted, all close together, in soil so foreign to them, that they had simply given up. They now waited, like tall but fragile guardians of something that would not be kind.

It was particularly unnerving in there as nothing stirred, the pine-needle thatch having suffocated any form or hope of life or regrowth. But they came out the other side without misadventure.

Next they encountered the area of deep holes and pools from which the humans had harvested the stones, rocks and minerals they treasure. Many of these had part-filled with rainwater down the years and they took great care to avoid the watching eyes of dragons, crested newts and toads that called this their home for fear that the reptiles, notorious for their fluctuating loyalties, would notice their passing. But the frogs were certainly too busy wrestling with each other to pay them any heed.

There now remained one last hurdle on their journey, the Sky Lark meadow, which acted as a living moat around the sanctum of the mid-forest, the Greene Man's domain.

While they paused to plan beneath the rotting bough of a long-fallen ancient elm, Zephyr heard something move behind them.

"Quiet," he gestured, by holding a long index finger to his lips. He then pointed to where a black fox was slowly zig-zagging across their scent trail a short way behind.

"It is Vulpe," he whispered. "She cannot be trusted, especially not here. We must go."

But as they made to move on, Alice noticed that

something was wrong. As she patted the spider silk holster, she realised, with horror, that it was empty.

The Willowand had gone!

Vulpe, the vixen, was, like most foxes, full of versatile cunning.

Foxes are neither dogs nor cats, neither weak nor strong, neither fast nor slow. They are, in many ways, the best of all those animals and tread a fine line between most things, including the so-called forces for good and ill. That is the secret behind their survival. And foxes are to be found all over the round world.

When the werewytch had traded several unmolested winter trips to her chicken coop to visit the plump ladies without reproach, bar a future call on her services, Vulpe was aware of the bargain being struck. But she had pups to feed and was now doing this role alone, since the humans had cruelly hunted and then slain her mate. She could still recall the sound the pack of dogs made when they caught him.

The fact that the wytch then approached her with the task of tracking the woodland nymphs, however, was a surprise.

Balance in Ashridge Forest was a delicate thing and the mystical folk normally kept themselves to themselves.

Yet, here she was, on their trail and tasked with sounding the alarm (for what she had no idea) upon finding them. And, from the freshness of their scent, it would not be long now.

The vixen slunk even lower, her sable brush tail sweeping the ground behind her as, guided by her sensitive nose, she glided along the trail. Within a couple of dozen silent steps, she approached the landmark elm tree where the tiny mystical fellowship lay concealed. Then she felt the moonlight sky darken.

Her vulpine instincts warned her to roll, and she did, narrowly missing the vicious claw of a ghost raptor.

As she tumbled and twisted, more assailants zeroed in on her position and the air was alive with their screeching attack calls.

The ghosts of the forest were formidable foes, especially in numbers impossible to counter. So she turned and ran, snapping at the air as they continued to dive-bomb, aiming at her ears.

She arched her back as she felt talons tear into her ruff then leaped as she ran, dislodging her attacker. Finally she could use the tree cover as protection and the nymphs heard the cracking of branches and twigs for some time as the frightened fox fled.

The owls didn't stop to receive any thanks due. They were famously aloof, as all owls are, and not the sociable kind.

But one did swoop over Alice as it passed with phantom-like wings, to drop off something it carried.

She waved to him as he turned and whirled away with an ear-piercing cry that doubtless set many a mouse aquiver.

Then she bent down and replaced the Willowand in the sheath about her waist before it decided to stray again. As she did so she noticed that all had become deathly silent since the owls had departed.

There was not even a vague rustle to be heard in the leaves, not a breath of a sound.

They began their onward journey to this backdrop of a silence that, if it were possible to do so, actually grew as they crossed the grass moat towards the royal copse of interlaced yew and oak.

Songbirds slumbered in their ground nests, brooding cleverly concealed eggs. Even the shrews and voles, usually so busy in the smallest of hours, seemed to be tucked tight away tonight.

Only Sylvane seemed unperturbed by the unmistakable force they could all feel as they approached the sentinel trees.

Her family were tree-life specialists, a very important role within woodland nymph society.

They are especially sensitive to the needs and the feelings of trees and plants and she could sense the warmth and energy in this gathering space upon the slight rise.

The crescent moon was positioned directly above giving everything a dream-like feel, as they tentatively crossed the threshold.

It took a while for even their magical eyes to adjust, but what they saw then filled them with awe.

For there, standing on an island in the middle of a crystalline pool, its mirrored surface highlighting every magnificent detail, was the noblest and most radiant being any of them had ever seen.

Everything about the space he occupied and touched seemed fertile and rich, bathed in a soothing and nurturing, gilded light.

"I have been expecting you."

He spoke in a voice that didn't so much travel across space but ran straight down each individual spine.

"But I know the news you bring is not what I had hoped to hear."

The werewytch howled her disappointment and derision when the pulse of her incantation spell was broken by a positive power surrounding the owl mob attack.

She was furious, and in her wretched anger threw over the dark, three-legged pot, spilling its hissing contents onto the cabin floor where it sank into the thirsty old boards.

"That filthy vixen must have alerted them somehow," she cursed. "I shall see to it that those pups starve for what she's done."

Then she realised the consequences of her temper and that she would no longer be able to track Henry's progress either. Her third eye would be blind for the night and this didn't help her humour at all.

She drew her dark shawl about her and flew from the cabin in a hunched rage.

Perhaps a check of her animal snares would throw up something else for the pot.

As she disappeared in a hurry, Nimbus, undetected in the dark rafters, gingerly made his way down to the table. Then he noticed that there was something else inside the bunch of rags that she had taken from the back of the chimney stack.

He opened the folds carefully and came across a leather-bound black book. It was a fairly unassuming kind of a book, but something about it made him look closer.

He moved it towards the fire so he could see better. Opening it carefully, right on the preface page, was a picture of a tattered ship, barely afloat on a fierce and very angry sea. But that was it; the rest of the pages, although old and well thumbed, were blank and empty.

Flipping back to the cover, there appeared to be writing embossed on the front. But the years of soot and grime had partially obscured the words, making them hard to read.

So the brave nymph took off his bright green neckerchief, dipped it in a pot of water he found by a fireside chair and started to carefully rub away the dust and the dirt.

Eventually, he could make out a sentence in gold leaf, which read:

The Legend of the Lost
The tragic tale of a family, of love and of hope.

But, as he paused to take in what he had just read, a creeping sensation warned him that he now had company and was no longer alone.

Book 3

Voyage of the Romany Soul

Back at the village school the nastier children had laughed at him in human form for as long as he could remember, called him "slow brained", "stupid" and, worst of all, "special needs" just because he was quieter and therefore different.

Well, if only they could see him now, in his true form as he ran miles without catching his breath, bounded over the highest of boulders with ease and, with one call, summoned up his friends, his pack, his gifted like minds.

Now that was being alive; that was being popular for what you truly are; that was power.

Alice tried everything she could to get more of a response from her willow companion, hoping that the enchanted wand would be able to tell them more about Hearne's quest.

However, it remained stubbornly lifeless for now, as if resigned to fate.

Dianah was ashen-faced and Sylvie almost hysterical, tears streaming down her lovely face.

"But we are just a few tiny, faerie folk, Di. How can we be expected to carry the fate of the forest on our shoulders?"

"We have to remember what Hearne said about destiny," Alice said, speaking slowly and softly, almost as if she was trying to convince herself more than anyone else. "Everything about these events is happening for a reason; it has a purpose."

"And our purpose, right now," said Dianah, "is to get to that meeting place, across the Chalk Downs at the crest of the Fireills…"

Savannah didn't surface from beneath the waves while Holly waited, so she half ran, half flew down the rocks back towards their crystal cave.

The tide was much higher and had cut off the entrance, but she was soon skimming over the foaming white horses, through the foliage curtain and into the magical space.

There, she was hugely relieved to see, was her recently fallen friend. She appeared a little scratched and battered and bruised but she sported a smile as well.

"I am so pleased to see you, sister. I was just about to come looking."

Holly could see Savannah's battle scars healing as she spoke, the cave and pool working their wonders.

"I see you've discovered more today than just the watching wild ones," she said gently, gesturing towards Holly's wings.

Almost as if embarrassed, Holly landed and she rapidly changed back to the girl she was used to, in the batting of an eye.

"It seems there's quite a lot you haven't told me," she grunted, almost grumpy, as if the not knowing was the real issue and not the inexplicable magic.

But soon they were both sitting side by side, sipping

a warming sea tea Savannah prepared from an oddly delicious seaweed infusion, warmed by a spring she hadn't yet noticed, which bubbled and slightly steamed.

"That water comes straight off the Fireills, which run half the length of the country and also a very long way under the sea.

"Those hills are responsible for bringing thunder and rain on land, and warming the sea to bring food for the sea creatures.

"But you should see the odd life that spawns near the gaseous outlets," Savannah explained. "Comes in useful for warming drinks too."

"Tell me," said Holly. "When did you know that I had... you know... special... powers?"

"Couldn't you feel the connection between us when we first met?" asked Savannah.

"I knew when you saved me from drowning that you were my sister, the dark-haired, headstrong, clever one in the fisherman's tales.

"All was confirmed for me when I found you with the Moonstone and when I listened to you talking in your sleep when you were taken ill."

"But I had a fever."

"Yes, but when you spoke, you also spoke in the ancient faerie tongue, a language impossible to make up, to fake or to disguise."

"But how do you know?" Holly blurted struggling to get her head around what she was saying.

"Well, Holly, can't you tell? Why, we're speaking it right now."

It was only when she forced herself to slow down, to measure each word and to make the effort to think again in English, that she confirmed for herself that, yes indeed, when she and Savannah spoke like this, not only was she talking in that magical language but she was thinking in it as well.

Right now, what both girls were thinking was that they needed to start finding some answers that would make recent events start making some sense.

They had clearly run out of clues. Now the answers they were seeking were going to have to be uncovered in the riddle of the legend on the cave walls.

Time and tide, as the saying goes, wait for no-one.

So, while the sisters were lost in their thoughts, they hadn't noticed that the weather had changed much for the worse.

A hurricane had blown itself off course and now trespassed on the British Isles, their little island in the North Sea.

As the storm came up and over parts of Africa it carried part of a great desert with it, throwing orange sand into the air that momentarily turned the sky a misty russet hue.

All faerie folk and fisherfolk knew this for a bad omen.

The last time it had happened, the storms raged for two weeks, nearly starving and bankrupting the poor villagers of Mousehole, Helston, Porthleven and Coverack, for no boats could set to sea for fear of drowning in the waves or getting lost as no stars could guide them.

Holly was the first to notice her skirt becoming wet as the dry patch of the sand in the cave started to disappear.

"I haven't seen it like this before," said Savannah, clearly concerned. "Wait for me here, Holly. Don't try to fly out as the mouth of the cave will be blocked by now."

Sure enough, when Holly pulled back the stringy seaweed and seagrass inner curtain, she couldn't see any daylight at the mouth of the cave any longer. It was lit solely by the light given off by the pool and the enchanted sea shell lanterns surrounding it.

By the time Holly had examined the deepest recesses of the cave for any possible alternative way out (she wasn't the sort of girl just to take "can't" for an answer), Savannah was resurfacing, a string of seaweed in her hand. She gestured for Holly to join her in the water.

"This is a string of mimnr, or what the villagers call mermaid's purses."

"I know," said Holly, puzzled.

"Well, what you won't know is that each capsule contains a dogfish egg. When you change to Holly faerie form, each one of these will enable you to breathe, with me, under the water, for around ten mermaid minutes."

"Really?" said Holly, looking a little apprehensive at putting that string of slime anywhere near her mouth.

"Well, best give it a try then."

"Open wide and follow me," gestured Savannah, placing the first capsule in Holly's mouth as she pressed the clasp on the robe.

The taste was surprisingly pleasant, like a toasted fishfinger sandwich but with a little too much salt.

Under the water it wasn't quite as calm as she had expected. Looking up towards the pale turquoise light, she could see the impact of the waves crashing and how the small fry and debris were thrown back and forth as if in some sort of demented tumble dryer.

At first she was expecting to resurface pretty quickly. But she soon found that her wings worked surprisingly well under water and, while she couldn't match her sister for speed, she was no sea snail either.

Savannah, who was majestic like a bejewelled dolphin under water, smiled reassuringly and, to Holly's great surprise, spoke, her voice tickling at first, as it appeared straight inside her ear as it couldn't carry through the water.

"As we're here together at last, I want to show you something special," she said, which Holly thought was an odd turn of phrase as, right now, everything was *so* special.

To the left of her, a line of lobsters was marching on the rocky seabed, heading somewhere with very serious intent.

To the right of her, cuttlefish pulsed, changing colours like neon traffic lights as they danced between fronds of waving seagrass.

They were pursued by a school of large, grey fish with supper in mind but struggling with the magical camouflage.

Then, in a small, dark cave, two white globes threatened to betray an octopus or perhaps a long and cable-bodied eel, lying in wait for either party to stray close enough.

Savannah was leading them expertly along the long

ridge of rock, heading steadily further down until Holly felt a lump rise between her lips and into her mouth and start wriggling about. She realised it was the dogfish hatchling, so opened her teeth and then lips and watched it swim off for cover, casting the suspicion of a dirty look back at her as she positioned the next in the chain between her lips and started breathing freely again.

The current was with them as they swam and soon Savannah was slowing down at what, at first, looked like a large outcrop of granite or similar rocks.

When they got closer, however, Holly could see what looked like a large ship's wheel and fossilised wooden barrels on what was clearly an ancient deck and, near the bow, a distinctive bronze plate with a still-visible name:

ROMANY SOUL

Her jaw dropped and she was so stunned that she nearly swallowed her breathing aid.

For, if she wasn't mistaken, this was the very same ship that formed the centre piece of the legend in Savannah's cave.

Then that could only mean one thing.

Even though they couldn't be further away in this strange place, the sisters were closer to unlocking the mystery of their real home than they had probably ever been.

While Holly blinked in awe and wonder, Savannah had swum down to the hull of the ship, where several planks had clearly impacted with something hard, doubtless the cause of the wreck. Where they split, however, also provided an easy way in and she called Holly to join her.

Fluttering through the water on her glittering wings, purple-tinged under the sea water, Holly glided through the gap and was surprised to see her sister climbing into what must have once been the captain's cabin.

Somehow, an air bubble had become trapped here and was replenished by a small stream of oxygen-laced and perfectly breathable air bubbling out from the seabed.

So Holly carefully opened her mouth and let the second dogfish hatchling swim off, its job done.

"The hills don't just breathe fire," Savannah smiled. "Now allow me to show you the true crowning glory."

Her voice had gone up a pitch or two, she was so excited.

She lifted the large oak lid of what looked like a chest but probably doubled as a bunk. Reaching inside she came out with a chest within the chest inscribed with a very ornate letter T in an ancient and unfamiliar font.

From a shell purse about her waist, she removed a glittering key and used this to open the smaller chest.

She then, ceremoniously, lifted two items from the chest and presented them to Holly on her outstretched palms.

Holly recognised the largest item immediately. It was the legendary pendant necklace to which their Moonstone belonged, the empty space flanked by a diving dolphin in mother of pearl and a horned seahorse, rampant.

It was surprisingly light for something containing so much precious metal and intricate carving.

When she held it up to the seashell lamps that Savannah had lit for them to guide their way even under water, it radiated a prism of the brightest of light. It wasn't just returning what was shone on it but seemed to have its own inner light source.

Savannah then handed her sister the other item, a ring of darkest obsidian serpentine rock, found only in Cornish waters. Coming from the Culm Measures, a magical ridge of stone, serpentine was rumoured to contain great power.

This ring had been fashioned by very skilled hands into the shape of a Cornish raven in mid-flight. Tiny emeralds were set into the sockets of its eyes and the natural veins of the rock formation gave definition to the wings, creating the illusion of movement, of flight.

"This must be the black bird in the picture on your wall," Holly announced, in an excited voice.

But the sound of a stranger answered back. "That may well be, missy, but this ship is our prahperty makin' that there 'oard ours.

"Unless you wantses somethin' nasty to 'appen 'ere, I suggest you hands 'er over."

Savannah blamed herself for them being caught completely unawares.

She had become so excited at the prospect of sharing her find with her sister, finally able to start connecting some of the pieces of the great puzzle, that it had dulled her other senses and she had let her guard down, for once.

To be fair to her, nobody could have anticipated that sea gypsy pirates would find the wreck so far off shore, or would have mastered the ancient arts of breathing under water, known to none but the faerie folk. It was then that she noticed the miniature oxygen tanks and rubber fins that they had clearly removed to slip through the hole in the hull undetected. At least that put one magical mystery to rest.

Somehow, they must have been watching them.

"Royt bitta luck it waz spotting yer lights 'n' bubbles over here," said the leader of the group of four, who spoke with a strange accent, a sort of blend of rural farmer, rough Irish brogue and auld English Brummie.

"Ad Ziggy not made a wrong turn on account o' the storm stirrin' up the seabed, we mayz never a sithee."

"Look, we aren't looking to cause anyone any trouble," started Holly. She could feel her ears starting to burn with determination and anger bubbling up, but she fought hard to keep in control.

Savannah was pleased that both girls had taken on their full human form while exploring the wreck.

"We don't even know who you are," said Holly. "Sorry if we've caused some sort of offence but…"

She was interrupted, however, by the youngest and smallest of the men, the one with a long scar on his cheek, staring at her and pointing at a picture Holly had not yet had time to notice fully in all the excitement since arriving.

"'Tis her and 'tis them, oy swear 'tis."

He was waving his arm between the painting and the girls until the leader moved closer to the picture with his snap lantern.

He held it up and, yes, sure enough, there in the group of two adults and four children were two of the girls.

They were dressed very differently in the family portrait. But, drawn to their fine, chiselled features, heart-shaped faces, one with hair the colour of milk opal and the other like serpentine itself, there was no mistaking their likeness, no mistaking it at all.

"The children of the storm," he mouthed, as if he had seen a living ghost.

For perhaps that is, indeed, what he was staring at in that mystical place, beneath the waves.

By the time they surfaced, back on the beach, the current storm had blown over and the attitude of the gypsy pirates had changed like the weather.

Gifted a bag of old gold from the chest and a trinket or two each, they couldn't do enough for the sisters. In fact, they were bowing and scraping quite comically at times, appearing completely in awe of them both, which may have had something to do with witnessing their transformation into magical form to swim back up.

Nelson, their charismatic leader, handsome in the black boots, trousers and striped top he had changed into, seemed particularly taken by Savannah. She clearly wasn't oblivious to his charms either.

Holly was more than a little irritated by the sudden intrusion into their private mystery. But she too had to admit that it was a relief to have allies, of sorts, now. Especially when they discovered what surprises Nelson had in store.

As they sat around their cave campfire that twilight, faces glowing and highlighted by the crackling flames, the men took turns to recall and recount the myths and legends that surrounded the girls' family.

Much backed up the stories they already knew but they also learned that the sea gypsy clan were the remains of the loyal Cornish workforce of their father, Lord James Trelgathwin.

"He was descended from what was believed to be the original nomadic Celtish settlers in Cornwall," said Ziggy, in a hushed tone. "It was a land so tough and brutal at that time that only the strongest, bravest and wisest survived.

"Yet James had not only survived, but had met and married a beautiful wife, Elouisa.

"She was the sole child of a mysterious, some say wretched woman who, otherwise, lived alone in the woods.

"Her mother was believed to possess strange and dark powers. She, it is said, could even heal the desperately sick and restore the weak, if the price was right and she was so inclined.

"But, fearing she would be abandoned by her daughter, the mother did not approve of their marriage. She banished her daughter from her sight for betraying her and spent many years living a solitary existence in the dark woods.

"They never saw her and focused all they could on cultivating their land and growing their fleet of handsome, red-sailed fishing ships so that all would prosper.

"The settlement indeed thrived and became a village and they were blessed with children, four girls each so alike but unique in their own part.

"Then, one dark spring night, quite without warning, Elouisa's estranged mother, otherwise forgotten, wandered into their settlement, the small fishing village now known as Mousehole.

"She had never ventured from the woods before and her arrival caused the villagers, a suspicious and cautious people by nature, great alarm. They hid and shuttered their windows, barred their doors and sent their children to bed.

"The now-elderly woman was still beautiful but there was something dark about her face, hiding behind her eyes.

"She first made her way through the corn fields before stepping aboard a small fishing boat, which, it is said, without aid of either sail, wind or oar glided slowly to the mouth of the port our ancestors had worked so hard to build as a shelter from the worst of the weather.

"There, without dropping anchor, she came to a rest and waited. She remained there for many days, although it was hard to judge days as the sun did not break clear of the clouds that whole time. While she waited, the tide did not ebb, nor did it flood.

"After the first few days, the crops in the fields began to fail, turned brown, then black, then dropped, with their disease, into the soil.

"When the villagers became brave enough to venture out to vent their frustration, the fishermen would not launch their boats for fear of the dark shape at the mouth of the harbour and the strange behaviour of the sea, which they believed to be cursed.

"Elouisa and James took their own boat out to see her mother. But when they arrived they found nothing but a heap of black rags suspended from the mainsail beam, and a note.

"This simply read:

> *Now return what you have stolen*
> *to the powers that be*
> *lest thou suffer for ever*
> *the worst of me.*
> *Then nowt but savage shall thy fate see.*

"James was furious and before the onlooking villagers, in a rare fit of rage, burned the boat and everything in it.

"But from that night and for every night onward, the worst sea storm ever blew in, clouds arriving like feral black cats to haunt and harass the modest folk of Mousehole.

"No ships could be launched and many a great sailor died trying in vain, including some of our ancestors.

"James even took his best men and tried a jump launch from the harbour wall. But they all but drowned were it not for the safety lines.

"Mousehole was now completely cut off from other villages by the treacherous weather in the valley.

"What with the failed crops and no fish to be had, people survived on rock limpets, mussels, shore crabs and whatever they could scavenge.

"But in the end, the mood of some inevitably turned. And it turned against the Trelgathwin family.

"One particularly dark night, a group of the villagers,

armed with a pack of mangy dogs driven half mad by starvation, stormed the Trelgathwin family home.

"A fierce fight ensued between the mob and those who remained loyal to Lord James. They fought hard but there were just too many and the position became hopeless.

"After subduing them, the villagers allowed the family to pack a few trunks of possessions, then they marched them down to the harbour where James's ship, his pride and joy, was docked."

"The *Romany Soul*," cried Holly, hands to her mouth.

"Indeed," whispered Ziggy, his cruel scar glowing a little with the excitement of the telling.

Nelson picked up and continued the tale, his voice also soft and respectful, like he was talking in church.

"The family were ushered aboard by the angry group of Mousehole villagers who had hog-tied Lord James' loyal men, hungry hounds snapping at their heels.

"Faced with no other choice, the father and mother secured their children below decks. They wrapped them in the blood-red cloak Elouisa always wore and comforted them as best they could.

"Between them, the adults then mustered as much sail as they could handle before steering that beautiful golden vessel straight down the throat of the hellcat storm where it rose once, high above the gaping crowds, but then disappeared beneath the gigantic waves never to be seen again.

"That was also the last seen of the family. The last, that is, until now. And we should knows."

"Why?" blurted Savannah, forgetting herself at the excitement of knowing.

"Why? Well, you see, we were there, that fateful night many, many moons ago," said the pirate leader. "And so, oh fair one, were both of yous, I reckons."

It is a well-known fact that the werewytch kind can sniff out faerie folk as certainly as a hungry child can taste a chocolate cake in the air while it is still baking.

Back in the dark cabin in Ashridge Forest, Mother paused at the threshold, an unmistakably sweet scent invading her nostrils like a footpad creeping through the fog.

She gave nothing away but for that pause, simply hung the brace of young dead rabbits on the hook in the pantry then made her away over to the shelf in the opposite direction of the now closed book.

However, out of the corner of her eye, she could see the heat pattern of the errant nymph hiding under the table, following him as he darted quietly between objects, making for the still available crack in the door.

As we all know, Nimbus, despite his name, is not the nimblest of sprites. While weaving between a footstool and chair leg, he tripped over the lip of the carpet and before he hit the floor was held fast in the jaws of a foul-smelling white ferret.

"No point wriggling," the woman taunted him in her tired voice.

"Faustus has you fast and your magic has no dominion here," she laughed, drawing back the carpet to reveal the witches' magical pentangle etched into the wood, just showing through the dust.

"It is just as well he's been fed tonight or you would have been quite a satisfying meal," she cackled, poking him in his wriggling belly with a long-nailed, bony index finger.

Then, almost before he could blink, Nimbus found himself unceremoniously bundled into some sort of large pickling bottle (judging by the overwhelming vinegary smell). He was relieved if a little alarmed when she then punched holes into the lid with a knife, allowing him to breathe.

Now, when she peered at him through the glass, her face appeared cruelly distorted.

But he could still see the beauty behind her eyes, although worn down by the heavy burden of a deep and obvious sadness.

"You and I are going to have a very long conversation very soon," she threatened. "But first, we must eat."

And with that she covered the jar with something that blocked out all the light and set it down on a shelf with a thump, leaving Nimbus to fret and sweat whether that something she meant to eat would, in fact, be him.

Mermaid Cottage was a welcome sight when the girls approached it again under cover of darkness.

The family car wasn't there. So, using the key hidden in the faux wooden chest of the plaster garden gnome, Holly let them both in.

They were surprised to find the cottage empty.

On the table was a note in her father's scribbled but ornate hand:

Darlings, I have had to leave in a hurry.

I have tried to keep our precious peace.

But once we saw Savannah and the Moonstone together, we knew that the rest would fall into place for you quickly as it has, once again, for us.

I know now what I must do and we have to return north to fulfil that part of our family's destiny.

We didn't know when you would return but, with Savannah at your side, I know the two of you will be safe and secure here until we make it back.

Be gentle with NJ.

I love you and we will be together again sooner than you know.

P x

There was a creaking on the stair.

Holly's heart jumped as she realised it was Nanna Jo, red from rubbing her eyes, either from tiredness, worry, crying... or all three.

"Darling girls, I can't say how very, very happy I am to see the two of yous safe and well, come here."

She threw out her arms, bedspread attached, and encircled them in her loving embrace.

Several minutes of excited chatter followed until, suddenly, Holly remembered that they weren't alone.

Crossing quickly, she unlatched the top of the stable doors and with a flourish introduced the small gathering of rakishly clad companions outside.

"Nanna Jo, please allow me to introduce Nelson and his sea gypsy clan."

They all bowed theatrically towards the figures framed by the light in the door and were a bit disappointed when Nanna Jo, embarrassed by her state of undress, simply said, "Well you had all better get in out of that chill wind before you wake up all the neighbours.

"I'll put the kettle on the range, but heaven knows where we'll find enough milk."

And, with that, Nelson, Ziggy and another seven souls wound their way into the cottage.

"Well, seldom have so many 'andsome Cornish fellas been seen in one room," Nanny Jo said unintentionally out loud with a smile.

It disappeared just as quickly when one with a grey beard and black neck scarf seemed to read her thoughts and winked.

"You know where the biscuits are, Holly, come on now, make yourself useful," she said, blushing and quickly changing the topic.

The talking started late and went on all the way through dawn, during which it soon became clear that the adults knew a great deal more about the Legend of the Lost than they had realised.

"Your father felt it best to keep it that way, child. For we lost so much during that terrible storm.

"Took him a very, very long time and much magic to come to terms with the loss of your mother and sisters during the worst of the storm, when the boat hit the rocks."

Nanna Jo looked grave with concern as she recounted those dark days.

"But we didn't lose our mother in the storm. Mama died from the sickness, shortly after Lucy was born, you know she did, NJ," Holly cried, clearly badly stung by saying the very words.

"Sally-Anne was my niece and she was also a wonderful mother to both you and Lucy, my gorgeous, brave girl.

"She was, however, your father's second wife. She helped him get over the loss of your mother, darling.

"So it nearly killed him to be robbed of two wonderful women in a single life time. Even though an enchanted and blessed Trelgathwin – or, as you know us, Savage – lifetime is a very different lifetime."

At this the various men, squeezed into every available nook and cranny, sipping their drinks and listening respectfully, nodded in knowing but concerned unison.

"But the legend tells of at least four sisters. So what of the other girl in that picture? Who is she and where is she?"

"Well," replied Nanna Jo, "That is why your father left so suddenly. Having regained the parts of his memory that he blanked out in pain, Savannah has given him fresh hope, something he never dared feel before." She smiled. "A day ago, news arrived at the cottage of something reappearing in Ashridge Forest."

"Near our home in Berkhamsted?"

"That's right, child. The omens were too hard for him to ignore so he has taken Lucy, and JJ of course, with him to seek out what it means."

"But they are heading into grave danger. There are things in the dark woods here and, I suspect, there, that mean us and all good and magical folk harm." Savannah rose to her feet as she spoke.

"We must go to him, he will surely need our help."
"I'm sure it can wait until everyone has rested up. It's a long journey by train; they don't run today and I did promise your father…"

At this, Nelson stepped forward and with a flourish announced, "Perhaps we may be of service again, ladies? Were it not for your father and your family, none of us would be here. We may have our faults but we owe him our loyalty and our troth and we travelling folk are nothing if not loyal in honouring an ancient debt of honour."

M adame Rebecca was the flamboyant matriarch of the sea gypsy band and she dressed to impress.

Wild floral patterns were coupled with a crystal and diamanté-encrusted tunic and lace-lined, billowing skirts in primary colours.

She kept a large knife in her belt, a warm heart in her chest but an ice-cool head.

She was clearly quite the eccentric.

Nanna Jo felt they were all going to get along splendidly.

"So, the legend has finally come to life. I guess you'll be looking to take the Aquavans then?"

"Aqua? Sounds like some sort of ship," enquired NJ. "Well, unless something dreadful has happened while we've been away, Hertfordshire is landlocked." She giggled at the challenge.

"But then you didn't consider the canals, dear lady," chirped Ziggy, flinching instinctively, expecting a flying shoe or swinging arm from Madame Rebecca.

"A genius plan," she snorted, screwing up her face. "If you have a taste for that stagnant canal water where ducks and all sorts do their dirty business."

Holly and Savannah didn't bother to question the merry band, as they were soon drawn down to the casting-off point at the foot of the ancient smuggler's pub.

A secret doorway concealed a boathouse that used to be the primary route for contraband and a way of avoiding the port authorities.

It was here that the strangest of vessels lay in wait.

Part boat, part Romany caravan and part submarine, Nelson and his sea gypsies were very proud of *The Changeling*.

It was deceptively roomy inside, a bit like the belly of a very large, wooden fish, and was powered by a blend of mystical mechanics. The craft drew energy from a bank of quartz blended with the sort of atomic rocks abundant on this coast. The rest was, well, a mystery.

Soon, they were gliding out of Porthleven harbour and heading north-east, where they would eventually intersect with the river and then the abundant canal system.

The journey promised to be a long one, in theory. But there was something about the manner of these merry men that calmed and reassured the girls that, despite the scale of the trip, they would get there in good time.

As Nelson pointed out when they asked, "Ever seen a gypsy caravan actually travelling? That's the thing with we ancient travelling folk, plenty of orn'ry people see us there when we're there. But who actually sees us getting there, eh?"

No doubt, magical gypsy time just isn't like the passage of minutes and seconds dictated by any normal wristwatch. So this trip was to prove, as no sooner had the passengers nodded off in their hammocks while they cruised quietly under the sea than they seemed to wake to bright skies and the neighing – yes, the neighing – of horses. And, no, not seahorses, because they sound very different indeed.

Outside was a hive of activity as men were hauling panels and parts off *The Changeling* and tugging at levers and turning cogs.

"Ah, glad you've woken up finally. You can see a sight few get the chance to," announced the sea gypsy leader.

And what followed had them fascinated. *The Changeling*, true to its name, was being transformed into a rather unique-looking, but completely serviceable canal barge. The whole process, using so many specialist hands, took less than one hour.

While this was happening, on the bank of the canal, four burly piebald ponies, just like so many you will now notice in fields up and down the country, "neigh, neeeeighed" with excitement. They pawed at the floor impatiently and longed to be getting on with the business of marching inland.

Tossing their shaggy black manes, stamping their hooves until sparks flew and whinnying with joy, they too seemed to know that adventures like this, even for mystical creatures, don't come around very often.

In no time at all the enchanted piebald ponies were harnessed to the barges and this colourful army of all sorts set off on the final leg of their journey.

Now they were travelling at an unexpected pace towards a destiny not entirely in their own hands.

The sisters tingled with an equal measure of excitement and pit-of-the-stomach dread of forces they still couldn't quite comprehend.

Deep in the forest, in the place human eyes seldom venture, through a thicket of gorse and bramble and devil's thorns, Henry sat and cleaned his heavy coat with his own tongue.

He loved the freedom that his true form gave him. But, sometimes, being a lycanthrope or, to use the name he preferred, weirwylde, had its drawbacks.

Fur balls and mucky tongues were no fun.

But, oh, the feeling of living in a world where every sight was so much brighter and clearer, every sound so much louder and every scent overpowering and delicious and alive.

Back at the village school, the nastier children had laughed at him in human form for as long as he could remember, called him "slow brained", "stupid" and, worst of all, "special needs", just because he was quieter and therefore different.

Well, if only they could see him now, in his true form, as he ran miles without catching his breath, bounding over the highest of boulders with ease and, with one call, summoning up his friends, his pack, his gifted like minds. Now that was being alive; that was being popular for what you truly are; that was power.

"Are we really 'hunting' berries and nuts again

tonight?" grunted a sulking Sam, the only one of their pack with a long ginger and silver stripe running down his ruff. "I would really like some flesh, just this once."

"Every time!" replied Oliver, the smallest of their number, showing his frustration.

"It's always the same story, Greytail. You howling about how hard done by we are, just because our ancestors took the 'no harm' pledge.

"Next comes the bit where you tell us that you get meat at home and one of us explains the difference between farming and wild spirits etc. etc."

"And then we eat," announced Tod Catchall, one of three young wolves to join the party slightly later, as he and his companions slid unheralded beneath the perimeter.

To snuffles and grunts of approval, they threw a sack filled with raspberries, blackberries, last season's hazels, ground nuts and loganberries into the midst of the gathered pack.

"Great. Now we don't even get to compete on the hunt for food tonight either," Sam moaned.

Tod just smiled as if to say "looks like you've lost there too". But he didn't, to keep the peace.

"Don't be so quick to judge, Sam, old friend," said Henry. "You don't yet know what we have planned for our pack. For the next few nights, the blood moon returns to the skies above our forest home."

"Meaning the curse – sorry, the pledge – is lifted until the old moon returns," replied Sam, the excitement building in his voice.

"Indeed. But, as you're well aware, we have an ancient debt of honour to uphold and there's much work to do.

"Something, as you know, is wrong with the balance of the forest and, unless we become part of the solution, the fate of our way of life, our homes and our families will be at risk."

Sam, however, had stopped listening. They now had the opportunity some had been waiting for since the teasing, humiliation and bullying first began when they each entered village school life.

The way Sam saw it, the villagers had made outcasts of him and his kind. He had put up with their nastiness for a very long time. He had turned the other cheek and all they ever seemed to do was slap that one as well and call him a fool for his trouble. He hated them and he hated school and he despised the bullies who tormented him with their idea of normal.

These evenings of freedom with the pack were his only release from that life. But now he was being told that was under threat too. It was all too much for his young mind to take in.

He now could only think of one thing, and that wasn't obeying some ancient order. It was revenge.

But that revenge, under the blood moon, would be red in tooth and in claw.

"Sam!" called Tod, noticing that he appeared distracted again. "Did you hear Henry? We're setting off on a trek, before dawn, to get to the bottom of the rumblings in the Fireills. That should be adventure enough even for a restless soul like yours."

"You go ahead. Let me catch up with you," he said. "First there's something I can't put off any more."

With that, Sam was away beneath the ring of thorns and off into the shadows of the forest.

Tod made as if to go after him but was blocked by Henry's intervention.

"But where's he going? I don't think we can trust Sam any more as I'm not sure he trusts himself, Henry."

"Sam is now in the arms of his destiny, my friend, and there is nothing that any of us can do to argue him from that path, no matter how we try.

"We can only control what is within our power and the gift of those who can help us.

"Our task now is to seek out allies and to do what we can to restore sense and balance.

"You know that too. Now come. Time is fast running out, for us all."

Nimbus may have been temporarily blinded by the black wytch, but his keen nymph ears could clearly make out the unmistakable noise of an approaching werebeast when he heard one. He was only thankful he couldn't smell it.

One thing his captor didn't seem to understand about their kind is how clever and industrious woodland nymphs can be, especially his clan.

His family were builders, architects and engineers. They made the things that made the faerie town the pretty, happy place it was. And he had been working on those holes in the lid of the jar for some time now, quietly convincing the metal edges, with a little help from his wand, to withdraw together, leaving a hole large enough for even his belly to squeeze through.

He had to work stealthily, for there was no way to mould magic without creating at least a little light. But he was counting on the fact that she had covered the jar in a dark cloth to conceal his efforts.

As he heard the door creak and his captor presumably step outside to greet her beastly guest, he seized his moment and popped from the jar like a cork from a bottle.

He then opened the latch on a rear window, made his way over to where the ancient, leather-bound book still lay, covered that too with the cloth and cast a replicant spell, taking care not to spill any light.

Then he re-covered the jar and tiptoed over to the window and climbed gingerly outside.

First checking that he was downwind of sensitive snouts, he made his way to the roof and along the wooden gutter until he could see the wytch talking with her visitor.

He looked like a relatively young werebeast and as the clouds shifted overhead to reveal a sliver of silver moon he noticed that, unusually, it had what appeared to be a white two-toned coat, a long streak of silver extending from neck to tip of tail.

He couldn't hear everything they were discussing but one sentence hung in the night breeze and froze the magical blood in his veins: "Revenge will come when we lift the curse of light by ending the reign of the Greene Man."

Just then, one of the winged forest ghosts glided past, catching the attention of the conspirators with its hunting call.

Nimbus seized the opportunity, with the house at his back, to fly hard and fast for the cover of the watching trees.

He had to find a way to catch up with Alice and his friends and share all he had learned in the cabin that evening.

For the wytch would soon discover that they were on to her and that would doubtless speed up her evil plans.

But as he darted between leaves, branches and

boughs, what was troubling him greatly was the puzzle about how much Alice understood about her own mother.

"Surely she must have suspected something?" he thought, panting under the strain of flying so fast for so long. If she did, what would that say about the true nature of their friend?

And, if she really knew nothing about her true nature, how on earth was he going to break the terrible news? It would surely break her heart.

Alice and her nymph companions had drifted through the audience with the majestic Hearne like they were in a waking dream.

It seemed both to last forever and to be over in a flash.

It was numbing and stimulating, exciting but frightening all at once.

She remembered every form of benign woodland creature parading by in a constant stream of tributes while they were in his presence. It was as if they were calling in to recharge their life source, worn down by nature's many tiring trials.

None of them could actually remember speaking with the prince of the forest. Yet he seemed to know precisely what they had come there to tell. He was in front of them and in their minds, their thoughts, doubts, fears and hopes, at the same time.

It was an odd yet a strangely comforting experience, almost like listening to a soothing lullaby on the shoulder of a loving parent.

And, as a result, as if surfacing from that waking dream, they were now trekking northward for the Chalk Downs, on a mission to search out and extinguish the source of the harrowing of the Fireills.

"I would do anything for him to protect our way of life. But I still don't understand how such a small band as ours is supposed to tackle evil in its very lair," said Sylvane, the natural fretter amongst them, pulling her pretty light green cap tighter as they flew against the wind.

"You heard his words as the rest of us did," replied Dianah. She had a bundle of thorn spears tied to her back, sword at her side and new bow. "Our mission and our help awaits us at the pinnacle of the hills, so it's to help that we're headed."

"But I was always taught that to break from the cover of the forest was fraught with danger," Sylvie countered. "I just hate being away from the trees. It never feels right. Our enemies multiply the further north we come into the Firewyld domain, and not all dangers crawl or run upon the ground."

"Well, you heard what he said, like I did," Alice said breathlessly as they flew. "Without risks we don't know what it's like to be safe and secure. Without hard times we don't appreciate the good…"

"Yes, yes, and without darkness we can't really see the light properly," repeated Zeph.

"It's the darkness bit that has me really worried, because there's dark with moonlight and lovely twinkling stars and the friendly bush folk…" Sylvane was clearly a little distressed by their mission.

"Then there's the dark realm those creatures inhabit, a place of hatred and fear and hurt," said Dianah.

"Well let's expect the worst and prepare to be

pleasantly surprised, shall we?" Just as the words left her mouth, Alice pointed at the horizon while they browed the first hill.

There, coming across the valley at incredible pace, was what appeared to be a band of emberhawks flying in hunting formation and they had clearly spotted the travelling companions.

"Talking of the worst... look! We're too far from cover now and they are much too fast," cried Dianah. "We need something protecting our backs." She pointed at the clay chimney pots on the farmhouse roof beneath them. "They will have to do."

They dived fast as one and positioned themselves between the set of four pots, each grabbing a spear and standing back to back in a sort of faerie folk diamond.

They were just in time.

The emberhawks were upon them before they could draw breath, three veering off in the face of the unexpected spear barriers and the attentions of Dianah's fast-firing bow.

The largest, however, circled back round and landed on the lip of one of the pots with an ear-splitting screech.

Its razor-sharp talons clack-clacked just above Alice's head, causing her to flatten herself suddenly in the middle of the pots, losing her spear in the process. She could feel Helygenn the Willowand wriggling in its sheath but it was pinned between her body and the clay roof.

Then she felt something like moths landing on her

face and realised that they were feathers, feathers from the attacking raptor.

Zeph had conjured an elven sword from his wand and, leaping nimbly this way and that, he was expertly carving chunks from the flight feathers of the winged terror.

Realising, however, that he had damaged its ability to fly, the hungry bird redoubled its efforts and, like the skilled predator it was, thrust its vicious beak between two pots.

It managed to grab hold of the hem of the sprite's tunic, despite his best efforts to fight it off, dislodging him from the security of the chimney in the same swift action.

Zephyr, however, cut the cloth with one action then, rather than push back as the bird expected, charged towards it.

Taking a feathery foothold, he then sprung onto its back.

This caused the bird to panic for fear of his slashing and stabbing blade, release its claw hold on the roof and attempt to take off.

The angry bird made a dozen more yards or so but then, in the face of the damage sustained and continual attentions of the nymph, crashed into an unseen washing line and cartwheeled, half dropping and half gliding, to the ground.

In the meantime, Dianah had sunk her spear into one of the returning birds far enough to encourage it to abandon them as a meal and clear off in search of easier prey.

The last, however, was proving a lot more determined, until Sylvie, with a wave of her wand, sent a shower of brambles from a nearby bush into the bird's startled face. That was enough to convince it to join its companions, screaming out its frustration as it launched awkwardly into the empty sky.

When the birds were far enough away to offer no threat of a return, the nymphs flew over to where the fight between Zephyr and the leading emberhawk had concluded.

They were expecting to see the bird slain on the floor. But, as they searched, their eyes were drawn upwards by a triumphant screech and the sight of the hunter heading into the horizon, lit up by the pale moon.

To their horror, it had a wriggling bundle clutched in its terrible talons.

At first the friends were set to chase the bird of prey. But, as Dianah pointed out, a look of horror on her face, "They simply fly too fast and it has too much of a head start."

"We can't just do NOTHING," cried Sylvane. "Can't you use the Willowand?"

Alice had already tried to get a response from her strange companion, however it remained lifeless, as if resigned to a fate it may well have anticipated.

Dianah was ashen-faced and Sylvie almost hysterical, tears streaming down her lovely face.

"We have to remember what Hearne said about destiny," Alice said, speaking slowly and softly, almost as if she was trying to convince herself more than anyone else.

"Everything about these events is happening for a reason, it has a purpose. Our purpose, right now, is to get to the meeting place, across the Chalk Downs at the crest of the Fireills."

"But how can we just…?" Sylvie said through her tears. "And we're just a few, little people…" She then broke down, sobbing.

The nymphs instinctively threw their arms around each other in a comforting, protective circle and held that position for what seemed like a very long while.

Although it was the hardest thing any of them had ever done, they eventually composed themselves and prepared for the final leg of their journey.

From the rooftops of the farm buildings they could see a glow appearing over the top of the Downs.

Some could mistake it for the fable of "red sky at night, shepherd's delight". But they knew there was nothing at all delightful about the omens surrounding a red glow over the Firehills.

Those hills were the very gateway to a wickedness that, if not stopped soon, would unleash unstoppable heartache upon their beloved land.

So the small party, painfully aware that they were so much smaller now, set off again, a gentler wind kindly lifting their gentle wings as they resumed the climb towards whatever fate had next in store.

Deep down in what the villagers jokingly, but depressingly, called the Valley of Doom, a long-disused factory lay rotting by a filthy quarry.

For decades this site had chewed up the land and poisoned the rivers, plundering nature without a thought to the feelings of the creatures that called it home.

So, eventually, when enough people plucked up enough courage, they ganged up on the company running it and they shut it down. The foul machines ground to a halt and life returned, slowly.

But soon reports were being received of strange creatures emerging from the swampy water, of foul and twisted beasts created by the mess left behind.

Most people dismissed these tales as fanciful scare stories, but not everyone.

Eventually, there were so many stories that the entire valley became a place that only the foolhardy entered at their peril. For, monsters aside, it was clear that the factory owners had not cleaned up as they should have and the land was now cursed and rotten.

The place was all but forgotten.

Until the incidents started.

Gradually, the poison started to spread in the water and in the air, as dark clouds bringing acid rain.

First it killed plant life and then it started harming the animals that lived in the lakes and pools nearby.

Many grew ill and then simply wandered off, never to be seen again.

Then reports came of strange, disfigured beasts raiding dwellings on the fringes of the forest, mostly late at night, carrying away crops and occasionally attacking woodland creatures or friendly faerie folk who got in their way.

The victims' tales were varied. But they had two things in common: the monsters all came from the valley of the Fireills and they all had a desperate, malign intent.

The night creatures signalled the witching hour as the tiny party of woodland nymphs reached the Sentinel Tree, an ancient and hardy yew that marked the valley's southern edge.

As they flew into its welcoming foliage, Alice noticed that it was only evergreen on one side now. The other was brown and bare. Despite its ancient power, it had clearly suffered as well.

This noble bough was the stuff of legend and had provided an important buffer to the sadness its roots could feel.

Sylvie was hugging one of its boughs tenderly and Alice could sense her wand tingling now, as if it were communicating with its woody cousin in a language none of them could hope to understand.

From this safe, sheltered vantage point, their magic was strong and the nymphs could survey large swathes of the valley for the first time.

But it was a view that both frightened and horrified in equal measure.

Compared to their forest home, there was so little growing here. The hillside was barren bar exposed rocks, clumps of brown and spent dirt. All the goodness had been bleached from its soul.

A dark brown, clay-like sludge oozed from the quarry pit.

It had been dammed off by the villagers at some point, presumably to stem the poison from spreading.

Yet nothing had been done to contain the steady trickle of effluent from its source in the hills.

This continued to spill over the lip of the makeshift dam, soaking into and tormenting the parched ground until it was dead and bare.

In the heat of summer days, a foul dust arose from this land, sending toxic clouds deeper down the valley or causing acid rain when the weather turned.

This burned the plants and trees and brought sickness and disease.

So the evil, poisonous plague of this place spread and spread.

While the friends surveyed this distressing scene of desolation, worse than anything they had allowed themselves to imagine, various hunch-backed, hairy and gnarled shapes shifted in the dark mouth of the disused factory.

An unnatural force was clearly gathering in the gloom and before long they realised that this was a greeting party for another nocturnal traveller from Ashridge Forest.

Emerging steadily from the path that scarred the valley floor was an entirely unexpected but unmistakable form.

Travelling to meet the malevolent creatures that dwelled in this desolate place, was what looked like an elderly woman. She was carrying a walking stick and clad in dark robes. She was also flanked by a snarling, striped werebeast. But it was walking upright, like a human.

That sickening image was chilling enough.

But, not far behind them, as if being born from the darkness that licked the fringe of the pit, were dozens and dozens of hideously twisted bears, wolves, badgers, polecats, boars and other deformed beasts.

"It's some form of filthy werebeast army," hissed Dianah, a little louder than intended.

"But… but…" Alice cried, through hands cupped to her mouth due to the horror of sudden realisation. "they seem to be led by… by…"

"Who?" her friends asked, voicing unanimous concern.

"By my mother."

Book 4

Ravenring

Everything about the beautifully twisted creatures at her command reeked of her malevolence and bleak revenge. They embodied her thoughts as they snickered, snarled and howled their way down the long-forgotten passageway connecting the darkest part of the dark downs to the centre of the castle, the former home of the Black Prince..

This vengeance had been decades in the making. And it would be all the more fulfilling for the torturous wait.

This would be justice for the outcasts, revenge against the race that had treated her own mother so cruelly, that had destroyed her own family and that had now abused, polluted and neglected the creatures of the forest and the fields where they lived.

The sea gypsy convoy had now grown into a ragtag mini-armada as it made steady progress by night, travelling up tributaries of the mighty Thames river.

Madame Rebecca and NJ were getting along famously and teasing the young pirates mercilessly as they floated fast.

Holly's mind, as active as always, was scrambling to try to put together the pieces of the very many things she had learned about their special family.

While she contemplated what may lie ahead at the end of this journey, she reached into the smart leather bag and took out the necklace and the ring.

She then took the Moonstone from her pocket, which was, as ever, vibrating slightly as it glowed.

"Try it there..." whispered Savannah, who, despite her ever-gentle tones, made Holly jump a little. She had been so wrapped up in the magic of the moment that she forgot her sister was in the corner of the cabin watching the strange world glide by.

Holly moved her hand towards the empty centrepiece, but the stone was almost drawn out of her fingers as she approached the necklace. It popped itself into place like a cork popping back into a bottle.

"Oh," exhaled Holly, a little surprised, realising it

was now fully secure, despite there being no clasps or other fixings.

Savannah smiled, somewhat knowingly.

Gradually, the radiance of the Moonstone spread to the rest of the necklace, like ink on blotting paper, until the whole piece glowed fabulously.

She handed the completed necklace to her sister, where it seemed to want to go.

After admiring it around Savannah's slender neck for a minute or so, Holly then turned her attention to the ring.

This was an altogether different affair. There seemed nothing special about the stone from which it was sculpted and the raven on the wing appeared relatively crudely carved.

But, when she placed it on her finger, something unexpected happened.

The jet-black bird seemed to fold its wings around her flesh and the ring tightened in a way that made her panic and quickly whip it off, like it was burning.

"Ugh!" she cried. "Something about that made me feel all peculiar."

Then a voice came from behind them.

"Well, the Ravenring isn't for little girls to play with," said the unmistakable voice of Madame Rebecca, who had been watching from the doorway. "Unlike the other potent relics and touch stones from your family, the ring can only really be worn by its bonded owner until they pass and hand it on.

"You see, the raven is the bridge between the

155

underworld and this world, between light and dark, life and…"

"The other," said Nanna Jo, bursting in with a tray full of cookies and hot chocolate. "There will be plenty of time for that dark stuff when we arrive. In the meantime, you girls need to keep your strength up.

"Mug for you too, Savannah. Anything's got to be better than that seaweed and sea cucumber juice you were telling me about earlier."

All laughed out loud at that comment.

Yet, while they sipped and nibbled and chatted nervously, none could help but notice that having three of the Trelgathwin treasures back together created a more optimistic atmosphere in the group. It also seemed to bathe the cabin in a faintly mystical, golden glow.

Up on the deck, Nelson had sent scouts ahead to ensure that they weren't sailing into some sort of trap.

He was becoming increasingly concerned at the orange glow on the horizon, which was lighting up more of the night sky ahead with every passing mile.

Several of the men had also reported a series of strange rustlings in the tree line and hedgerows that flanked them on both sides of the canal system.

Sure, more creatures come out at night than simple folk see. But there was something heavier than expected about the cracking of the branches and crunching of the leaf litter than could be dismissed as a badger or fox or even otter.

After all, that sort of nocturnal creature would have come out to greet them as they passed.

Yet they saw disturbingly few friendly faces.

Even the enchanted pulling ponies were starting to show their nervousness. And they were the bravest of beasts, said to have borne knights of old into battle.

"Well," said Nelson quietly to Ziggy, his voice hushed but ever confident. "Looks like we 'ave company. We canz but be ready for whatever fate may throw at us next, as we canz hardly turn around now, dear friend."

Without having to be told, Ziggy slipped off to warn the warriors up and down the quiet convoy to keep their wits about them, their weapons clean and their companions close.

Berkhamsted Castle is famous the world over for being the former home of the infamous Black Prince, a malevolent knight.

It is a handsome ruin, in the main. But it still sits proudly at the heart of the village, if you know where the true heart is, that is.

The castle's ancient and mystical all-seeing towers, despite being many centuries old, are still raised on steep grassy hills and banks, encircled by a shallow moat.

The canal meanders lazily by to the east, while Ashridge Forest, its closest neighbour to the north and west, is just a short march away.

It is said that the castle was built using ancient timbers cut from the ancestor trees in that sacred forest.

It is also rumoured that, despite the attentions of armies past and the ravages of many hundreds of years, within the castle's remaining flint walls, quartz and other magical crystals are still buried.

But the families camped out there this evening had little thought or concern for magic. They were too busy listening to the music of the natural world, the serenades of the bullfrogs, toads and bats that abounded there, though they knew not what they were saying, given that most of us have forgotten that ancient language of nature.

The group were also enthralled by the supernatural; the ghosts, ghouls and terrifying monsters starring in the fireside stories expertly performed by their mums and their dads camping with them.

And, while their parents took turns to titillate and terrify them, the youngsters huddled together, baking bananas with chocolate buttons and roasting marshmallows on long reeds or sticks.

All of Holly and Lucy's best friends were here, including Niamh, Reanna and Alex, back from the beach too, as well as Philly (and sisters), Max, Zack, Grace and Ellie.

Lucy recalled that, for as long as she could remember, Holly had organised this annual camp-out to mark the end of their summer holidays.

"How annoyed she will be to be missing this one now," she thought, just as Niamh's father pulled his face back and snarled, pretending to be a beast of some sort. Jack's snarl in response made them all giggle.

Her own dad was a bit more distracted than usual and wasn't leading the spooky stories as he so often did. He was clearly preoccupied with something he had not yet shared with his daughter.

But he took his turn when the other dads teased him into it and did a great job of imitating a rampant, multi-armed octo-beast on the hunt, although his beastie was more of a tickling machine than a child-eating one.

When they finally called it a night and slipped into

their tents and then sleeping bags, Lucy didn't want to press her dad too hard on whether Holly and Nanna would be back tomorrow.

They had been in touch, of course, to say that all was well and they were on their way. But a small part of her secretly liked the fact she was getting some one-on-one time with her pops.

With that warm and comforting thought and Jack snuggled in her lap, she was soon fast asleep, even before they turned out their lamp.

Her father, however, was obviously a lot less settled, with a heavy weight on his mind. He carefully unzipped his covers when he eventually heard his daughter's gentle breath settle into the rhythmic pattern that told him she was asleep.

He calmly and quietly pulled on his shoes. Then, after muttering what would have appeared, to those in the know about supernatural matters, to be a powerful guarding spell, he slid noiselessly from the tent and was swallowed up by the pitch black of the night.

The first attack came, unexpectedly, from the air.
One of the pirates at the rear reported seeing a large cloud, moving faster than the wind implied, blocking out what little moonlight there was.

Locking as many people as they could spare in the cabins and battening down the hatches just in time, the boats were soon swarming with millions of ferociously angry wasps and hornets.

Some of the men took to the water to avoid their myriad stings. The braver, or more foolhardy, quickly covered hands with gloves or clothing, faces with neckerchiefs or scarves and heads with hats or hoods, and scrabbled for the flaming torches.

Even the tiniest angry insects are formidable in force, but the flames and smoke deterred them for long enough to make it into a small road tunnel, thanks to the swift thinking of the piebald ponies. Interestingly, however, none of the bugs targeted them.

Nelson and a couple of men then set up barriers of fire at the entrance, while compatriots on the rear boat did the same at the back.

They could still hear the angry wall of buzzing wings and had to deal with those they had carried through.

But, with everyone springing to action once under

cover and the help of aerosols and the busy attention of wet towels and soaked coverings, they eventually contained the flying menace.

"Vicious mini beasts," exclaimed Ziggy.

"Something has clearly wound them up and pointed them in our direction," replied Nanna Jo, now dabbing ointment that Madame Rebecca had prepared from a bunch of herbs hanging in the galley area on the exposed raw spots of the growing number of casualties lined up for her attention.

"I'm not sure how long these barriers are going to hold," shouted Nelson, lighting another torch and throwing it to one of the female crew members.

As they all busied themselves with blocking or stomping the mini-beast peril, there was suddenly a flash of light and a purple, pink and red stream of stars flew through the flame barrier, heading outward.

The noise from the insects rose to a crescendo at this point and the wasps and hornets regrouped as a giant cloud promising overwhelming pain.

The cloud then started to climb high into the night sky: a long, vertical climb, straight up above the bridge.

The ponies, as if wanting to see the conclusion to the battle, towed the barges forward in time for everyone to witness what happened next.

Holly, in faerie guise, was leading the insects upward in a vertical climb.

She outpaced and outlasted the vicious horde.

Flying straight up, she knew that the altitude or

height would eventually take its toll. And it did, in spectacular fashion, as, after a few minutes, they heard a soft boom.

The sky soon lit up with gold and purple stars, like the best firework on bonfire night. It then started to rain insects, torrents of stunned insects dropping and hitting the water behind them like hail stones.

Not all of them met the same fate: some clever queens must have seen sense, judging by a large cloud from the rear of the swarm that pulled out, broke up and dispersed in all directions.

But it was clear that some clever thinking, fast acting and bravery had brought this battle to a swift conclusion.

What lay ahead, however, was anyone's guess. But, based on this incident, it was most likely the stuff of nightmares.

Alice watched her mother with a growing sense of disbelief and denial.

"How could she have…?"

The scene below them threw up so many questions she just wasn't going to find answers for here and now.

Her companions waited in respectful silence.

Sylvane in particular was feeling the heavy weight of her friend's discovery as if it were her own.

They had all been carrying the great burden of the news since the night of the attack on their glade, when Helice had warned them about reports that had passed to the elders from Hearne.

Part of the reason for visiting him was for him to see Alice for himself and confirm the link.

Dianah took the initiative and broke the shocked silence.

"Alice, you know that this does not mean that you…"

"What?" snapped Alice. "Doesn't mean that I'm a were-creature, a traitor, because my mother is the werewytch?"

Her face was contorted with pain and her eyes were brimming with angry tears.

"Well, that's such a relief, such comfort," she cried, storming off, unable to face her friends right now, still coming to terms with the fact that they clearly knew something about her own mother, her own family, before she did. She also felt such a fool that her mother had lied to and tricked them for so long.

So many questions now raced through her head in a few seconds. Most started with "what about": her brother, their friends, their home, their father, their loyalty, their safety?

She was so very upset, so very confused and so very afraid.

It was like everything she had ever known had just been placed on a rug next to her, then a giant, cruel, invisible hand had pulled it all from under her at once, breaking most things and alienating her from everything she had believed true.

It was then that she felt Sylvie's arm wrap gently around her shoulders.

Alice almost shrugged her arm off in her hurt temper, but she then changed her mind and surrendered to the love of her friend.

Sylvie always had a way with words and these were some of her best.

"Things may look bleak now, Alice. But things aren't always what they seem. We all make mistakes in life. But still the good you have flowing from every part of you must be in your mother too.

"For, after all, it was her and your father that together, made you. And, who knows, he may be searching for you too."

Then the tears really came.

Yet, sadly, as is the way in tough times, fate waits for no-one, no matter how hard the going gets.

So, even as the woodland nymph gang shared in the heavy sadness of their friend as if to carry some for her, the very object of their pain, the werewytch, was on the move once more.

Her dark conference with the creatures of the pit was clearly over as they were now being dispatched in various directions.

A large, mixed tribe of lycanthropes was heading off along the forest fringes for speed.

An evil air force of winged furies including buzzards, hungry land gulls and certain bats, ridden by what appeared to be hobgoblins, took to the air.

"I don't see any emberhawks," said Dianah, under her breath.

While those large groups set off, the bulk of the hideous army, now numbering thousands, clearly came under the werewytch's command and briefly gathered around her in a huge chattering, slavering, moaning mass.

To the surprise of the friends, she then signalled for them to follow and they made their way into the mouth of the quarry pit, the abandoned factory doors swallowing them greedily.

All went with her with the exception of the werebeast they had earlier seen by the werewytch's side. It turned at the last and broke away.

"Why would the largest group head back to cover? It looks and smells like hell on fire in there," asked Sylvie, giving voice to the question they thought at once.

"It may be that they draw some sort of poisonous power from there. Or perhaps the old factory is a wretched portal of some kind," said Dianah, with a worried look on her face. "If it is a bewitched doorway leading to somewhere they want to get to – fast – it is going to be nigh on impossible to track them."

Just then they caught a flash of light behind them and their hearts filled with instant joy at seeing the round, smiling face of Nimbus, beaming and panting, dragging a black sack behind him.

"Larks alive, am I tickled pink to see this jolly crew!" Nimbus dumped the sack on the ground in the middle of them just before three sets of arms mobbed him.

He then set about, as sensitively as he could, very much aware of Alice's feelings, relaying the recent events in the cabin.

First, making sure that they were well shielded beneath the Sentinel Tree, he then concluded by reversing the shrinking spell.

Suddenly the iron cauldron and black book bearing the title The Legend of the Lost both appeared, before shocked faces.

"I don't know how, exactly, but I have a feeling that these magical items are going to have quite a part to play in the fate of our forest."

He scratched the thick brown hair beneath his fawn cap as he spoke as if to echo his and their frustration with this terrible puzzle, on an epic scale.

This voyage of *The Changeling* had certainly been eventful so far and it was to prove even more exciting before the night was through.

When they left the outer clutches of inner London, a few of the watchmen had reported strange disturbances in the water.

At first they had put this down to particularly hungry nocturnal carp or barbell fish hunting by moonlight. But then it became clear that the ripples in the water were multiplying, and they appeared to be following them.

The first attack came as they entered a particularly shallow patch where the bank had clearly ruptured slightly, leaking a little.

They had just passed the clear water outlet from a sewage treatment plant and it was known that many a strange beast was to be found in those parts.

The helmsman of the rear boat heard a strange, plopping noise and then several more. Then, to his horror, the deck of his barge came alive with what appeared to be snakes, as thick as black cables.

They were trying to get into the engine compartment until several of the sea gypsies attacked them with brooms and sticks, forcing them back into the water.

"Eels; fowsans of 'em," he shouted, rousing more of his companions.

They doubled and then redoubled their efforts to get rid of the wriggling abominations. But there were just so many and, having burst through the doors to the engine bay, they threatened to choke up the drive machinery of the boats.

All appeared lost when the engines of the lead barges stalled, plunging them into darkness and leaving them drifting towards a grumbling weir, which would almost certainly have overturned the flat-bottomed boats had the ponies not pulled harder.

Then, suddenly, a golden glow started in the main cabin of *The Changeling*. It swelled steadily until, like a wave crashing on rocks, it burst over the barges and their passengers, both the real ones and the unwelcome boarders.

Almost instantly, the snake-like eels literally turned tail and vanished back into the oily water.

Within a few seconds, it was like they had never been there.

Then, with a sigh of relief, a quick wipe down, a tap or two on the engines and an urgent re-crank, they were soon on their way again.

The experience had been a shock.

"Nice work, Savannah," called out Madame Rebecca, who had seen her take mermaid form to enter the filthy water and perform the spell that returned the creatures to their watery home.

Her Moonstone necklace still throbbed and

glowed about her neck like the barrel of a smoking gun.

Savannah smiled back, although the effort had clearly taken a toll.

"At least some good came of that sneak attack," said Madame Rebecca, opening the large cooking pot boiling in the galley. She then dropped in a couple of the soon-to-be tasty beasts.

This did instinctively make Savannah wince a bit for she had such a close bond with all creatures that live in the water.

"Sorry, luvvie. But nowt blesses a marine gypsy's 'art s'much as a feisty eel," she explained with a grin. "Now les juz 'ope the next attack iz monkeys or some such an they'z frowin luvly fat tatties. Bout time we 'ad some decent veg."

They all fell about laughing at this prospect, missing the fact that the glowing on the horizon was starting to intensify from russet to blush red.

Nelson, however, had not taken his eyes off the horizon for some time.

Only once had he seen the sky take on such an unnatural colour. And that was many, many moons ago and all the way down in their ancestral village of Mousehole during that fateful night.

He was finding it hard to conceal his concern and noticed that his hand was shaking as he steered the travellers straight into the oncoming storm.

Still camped under the Sentinel Tree, three of the nymphs were trying to get the cauldron to work, while Alice studied the book, in quiet concentration.

"You do what?" shouted Sylvie, in marked disgust at Nimbus's suggestion that they had to swallow a phial of the rank potion then regurgitate into the bottom of the dark pot.

"We vomit it? Are you sure this will make us able to track them?" asked Dianah, clearly not convinced.

"Yes, I took some of her hair from her brush before I left so it will focus on her. And, yes… that's how you get the spell to work, Sylvie. I saw her do it."

Sylvie was holding up the phial of nasty-looking, sludgy soupy stuff when Alice looked up from the book.

With a wave of the Willowand, the phial spun in the air, circled the pot half a dozen times then emptied itself into the cauldron, on top of the hair that was already in there.

"That should give us a good few hours of viewing time," said Alice with a smile.

"How do you know that?" asked Nimbus, puzzled.

"The recipe is written down in here, silly, in invisiscribe, along with several other spells that might come in handy. Always pays to do your research properly.

The pukie bit is optional, by the way. It just saves on the effort of mixing and shaking."

Then they all laughed as Sylvie's face turned a green to match her pretty slippers.

No-one was brave enough to ask Alice what "invisiscribe" was or how she knew.

All eyes were soon drawn, however, to the surface of the cauldron, which bubbled and then moaned. It then gradually became clear, like the surface of the water on a clear, windless day.

At first they couldn't make sense of what they were seeing. And then it became obvious that they were watching hundreds of werebeasts of all shapes and sizes filing down what appeared to be a very long and dank tunnel.

It was lit by a greeny-orange glow that made it hard to see until your eyes adjusted. But the monsters were obviously in a hurry and very excited, judging by the snarls, snickers, cackles, growls and other bestial noises coming off them.

"That must mean there's some sort of passageway leading from the quarry…" started Dianah.

"Under Ashridge Forest itself," finished Sylvie.

"Which means they could enter the town, where the humans live, without any of our magical kind being able to stop them," said Nimbus, the implications suddenly dawning on them all.

"And if that happens, the ancient and fragile understanding between faerie and human folk will be broken," continued Dianah.

"I'm afraid so," said Nimbus.

"If something happens that not only tells all humans that we exist but also harms and threatens them, it will only mean one thing for us."

"Yes," said Alice.

"There will likely be a war between faerie folk and people.

"Just as we've discovered each other again after so very long, that would be a disaster for all of us.

"And the damage will be even worse than the pollution pouring from this nasty pit, that's for sure."

From their vantage point on the hill they could all see the orange, red, greeny light throbbing from inside the ancient factory doors.

It was an ominous sight, firstly because it most likely meant that nasty substance was probably bubbling out and scorching more of the earth, as well as causing untold other problems.

Secondly, and even more scarily, they all knew that, at some point soon, they would have to face what had just snaked through those gaping jaw doors, the pack of monsters marching through some sort of hell to start a war.

But even a magical cauldron couldn't possibly predict the fate that would be waiting for faerie folk and mankind alike at the end of that dark tunnel and, indeed, this tale. For, if they went to war, everyone, but everyone, would lose and their world would be cast into darkness forever.

S ea gypsies are a tough and loyal breed.

They are, after all, the descendants of the only villagers to remain true to the family when the frightened villagers cast them adrift in the magical storm.

They are the only people to have fought the prejudice of those villagers down the years, believing in the true heart of Lord James Trelgathwin, trusting that he somehow survived and questing to reunite with him and his family.

But when the third and most devastating attack came on their route to meeting at the castle, it tested even the famous resolve of the gypsies.

The first of their crew was taken around 2am.

She was on the landward side of the lead barge and was walking to the stern when something snarled and burst from the shadows, dragging her into the hedgerow and then bushes.

Before the rest of the crew could react, she had simply disappeared screaming into the dark.

The second attack came about ten minutes later when two men were knocked from the stern of the rear barge.

One alone just managed to claw his way free from the tentacles of something he never saw, thanks to the quick thinking of Savannah, who threw a shell into the water and blinded the attacker with an intense ray of magical light.

The poor crew member almost lost his senses and was now lying below decks whimpering with fear.

Nelson then doubled the guards leading the ponies. He instructed everyone else to light more torches to ensure there were as few shadows as possible in which evil could hide.

Savannah took to the water again and soon recruited a small navy of otters, water rats, mink, weasels, crayfish and even pike.

They patrolled the boats, just beneath the surface. Holly, assuming her faerie form, cast enchantments on the lamps so they shone as bright as daylight.

She also warmed the hearts of her companions with *delight* spells that uplifted their spirits by thinking warm thoughts, which kept them positive.

But, despite all of those precautions, no-one anticipated the fires.

As they began what Nelson believed to be the final five miles of their journey, they had to pass an area where aged wooded growth overhung the canal on both sides.

Holly flew into the boughs, scouting ahead, to investigate. But, seeing nothing suspicious, the barges moved forward, bunching a little on the water, where it was made narrower by the overhanging branches.

Suddenly, what looked like several shooting comets plunged into the bushes on both sides.

It soon became apparent that they were, in fact, some

sort of flaming insects and in seconds the dry brush was ablaze all about them.

The instant inferno caused even the brave piebald ponies, terrified of the flames, to panic, break free from their harnesses and gallop off across the fields.

All the barges in the flotilla were now stationary, sitting ducks, as there was no current on the canal and not a breath of wind.

Cinders and flaming shards rained down on the barges, setting fire to anything flammable and forcing all hands to scramble with buckets and wet rags to fight the flames.

While they were distracted, about a dozen macabre beasts leaped from the canal banks and onto the decks of the boats, howling and slavering as if possessed.

The pirates fought bravely, as expected, with Nelson and Ziggy dispatching three of them that had clambered onto the roof of the middle barge.

They used the punting poles as spears and forced the creatures into the canal, where Savannah's many water creatures made short work of them.

The fallen soon scrambled desperately back onto the banks and sank back into the darkness, tails between their legs, missing much of their fur.

Several of the abominable beasts had, however, managed to force their way through the wooden doors into the lead cabin where the ladies had been resting.

As others rushed to help they heard two gun shots rise above the sounds of desperate struggle coming from within, then several loud yelps and then silence.

Holly flew to the entrance as fast as her wings would carry her.

She arrived in time to see a pile of bodies in the sleeping area, including at least two of the werebeasts, one a twisted badger and the other some sort of dog-like creature.

But her heart dropped when she noticed what appeared, judging by her bright clothing, to be Madame Rebecca.

She wasn't moving.

Nanna Jo, on the other hand, was still wrestling noisily with one of the twisted animals.

She was clutching in both hands the barrel and stock of a shotgun that one of the foul creatures had bitten down upon, missing her face by inches and spraying her in beastly black dribble.

Without needing to think, Holly threw back the red cloak and, surging with the sense of courage it gave her, held up the hand on which she had earlier slipped the Ravenring. At the same time, in her mind, she pictured the monster flying through the air.

No sooner had the thought formed in her head than dark shapes emerged from the shadows beneath the bunks. For a fraction of a second, the room went deathly quiet. Then the shadows promptly set upon the beast.

The spectres formed by the ring adopted the shape of a flock of corvids: ravens and jackdaws and crows that filled the room with flapping confusion. This startled the angry creature.

In a blink of an eye they set upon and then pecked

the werebeast into submission. The terrible flock pecked away mercilessly until the beast just disappeared into thin air.

Then the phantom birds themselves slipped back into shadows.

"Nanna Jo," cried Holly, resuming her normal form as she spoke.

But Nanna Jo had thrown the shotgun to one side and was now cradling the seemingly lifeless form of the incredible woman who had been such an inspirational character in the little time they had known her.

"No, not you, Mother, not you," cried Nelson in a desperate voice as he suddenly slumped, breathless, through the barge door, clearly too late to help.

"She's still breathing," answered NJ. "But it's very laboured and shallow. Get these vermin off us and let's make her comfortable."

A couple of the crew threw the beasts' bodies overboard and between the three of them they managed to manoeuvre Madame Rebecca into one of the abandoned bunks and to make her comfortable.

The whole time they did this, battles continued to rage outside.

They were especially conscious of the continuing crackling of the flames both in the bushes and aboard the barges.

"I am going to have to get back out there or the same fate awaits all of us," said Nelson, before kissing his mother gently on her forehead.

"We will do everything we can, son, she's in safe

hands with us," said Nanna Jo, more in hope than confidence.

Then, with one backward glance, concern written all over his face, Nelson picked up the shotgun and then a blunderbuss from the locker before disappearing back onto the deck.

They could hear him shouting orders to the gypsy pirates to tend to the fires and then they heard several ear-splitting bangs as he put the weapons to angry, renewed use.

NJ gestured for Holly to rejoin the others as she busied herself with boiling water and the curious medicine cabinet in the galley area.

When Holly returned to the fray, she was shocked by what she saw.

One of the barges was so fearsomely ablaze that the crew were abandoning it, some still wrestling with mangy attackers on deck and in the water.

Several dark shapes lay slumped on the barges and banks. Here and there, members of the crew were tending to wounded colleagues covered in bites or vicious scratches.

Others were fighting fires or grouping together to drive off the most persistent of the monsters. And so it continued for some time until, eventually, the last of the evil beasts fled.

When the battle was finally over, the battered band gathered at the safe side of the canal, flanked by a long, low field with only a lock-keeper's cottage on the horizon.

Just the quiet calls of the night birds and the muffled moans of the injured disturbed the still air for a few good minutes until eventually Nanna Jo broke the silence.

"Well, there's some good news, at least. We wrapped Madame Rebecca in the Rubyrobe and her condition has improved hugely. She's sitting up now and cursing about the pottage potion we're making her drink. Her own recipe, I might add."

Although she managed a weak smile, Nanna Jo looked completely drained as she spoke, echoing how they all felt.

They were all acutely aware that they still had a fair way to go to reach the castle meeting point and unpredictable danger on all sides.

But, worst of all, none of them had a clear idea of what was waiting for them when they got there and, based on what they had encountered so far, they were starting to suspect the worst.

It was, however, clear from the attacks so far that someone or something really, really wanted to stop them getting to their rendezvous.

Someone was desperate to prevent the family and friends from reuniting, from reconnecting, from regaining the power of the love that was lost.

But Holly had a pretty clear idea now who that dark, dangerous and disturbed someone could be. And she was determined to overcome those plans.

The werewytch's senses were alive with the dark energy pulsating from the macabre army surrounding her.

Illuminated by the luminous, almost atomic light of the poisoned walls, they made fast progress through the gloom where miners had once worked like human moles.

Everything about the beautifully twisted creatures at her command reeked of her malevolence and bleak revenge. They embodied her thoughts as they snickered, snarled and howled their way down the long-forgotten passageway connecting the darkest part of the dark downs to the centre of the castle, the former home of the Black Prince.

This vengeance had been decades in the making. And it would be all the more fulfilling for the torturous wait.

This would be justice for the outcasts, revenge against the race that had treated her own mother so cruelly, that had destroyed her own family and that had now abused, polluted and neglected the creatures of the forest and the fields where they lived.

This was payback for the people who had forced her to live in exile, shunned by so-called normal folk.

The age of normal would soon come to an end.

Soon it would be the time of the misfits, the underdogs and the abused.

Once they announce themselves with great victory at the ancient castle, more and more of their tortured kind would join them, more would come.

Soon their army would grow to a force and then swell to the size of a nation.

Soon the abusive, cruel, greedy and neglectful reign of humankind would be over, once and for all.

Soon her long-awaited vengeance would be complete.

Alice and the little group of watching woodland nymphs had seen enough.

It was clear that they were going to be needed at the grounds of the castle, where this monstrous horde was heading.

Having spent some time studying the story and spell book, while it was difficult to decipher what everything meant and how it applied to these troubled times, it was apparent to Alice that the Willowand had an important part to play in what was to follow.

It was also clear that there may well be more to her little family than she had thus far realised.

This was something she had always secretly suspected.

She was also a little relieved by the legend. Her faith in her own mother had been sorely shaken by the events of the past few nights. It was causing her a lot of distress to see her at the head of the evil army.

What the book gave her was hope, hope that more was happening to them than simple good vs evil, that there was more of an explanation than was currently meeting the eye.

Sylvie, meanwhile, had summoned a small flock of long tailed tits as they were making plans. With that group of birds she had sent word of what they had seen and what they believed was taking place.

It was a small flock but they were many and they were very nimble. So she was pretty confident that the message would get through with them.

How Hearne and the elders responded, however, only time would tell.

For now, they would have to take whatever initiative they could think of if only to buy time until help came.

But, however they looked at it, what happened next surely involved this group of friends heading over the forest to Berkhamsted Castle.

So Nimbus eventually returned the pot and book to travel size and, with a last goodbye to the Sentinel Tree, they set off across the tip of the Chalk Downs and back over the dark forest.

"If we fly high enough we will be boosted by the thermal currents channelled through the Chalk Downs. Should get us there a lot faster than travelling along the ground," motioned Dianah as she climbed higher. "But keep your eyes peeled for raptors. This is where the red kites hunt, remember."

From above they could more readily see how the glowing effluent, the pollutant, was seeping from the factory site and leeching into the forest.

It was clearly burning and poisoning boughs, bushes and whole animal setts and burrows alike.

There could be little doubt that this pollution was to blame for creating whole families of twisted creatures tormented by its evil influence.

"How can the humans have allowed this to happen to our home, and theirs?" shouted Sylvie as they passed over an entire grove of elm trees that had shed their leaves in distress.

"Well," said Nimbus, "if they don't wake up to this soon, it very much looks as if we will all have to pay a heavy, heavy price.

"There will be a battle like none ever seen. Yet I really can't see how either side can come out of a war as winners."

Back at the quiet campsite in the middle of the castle ruins, Lucy and her friends slept soundly in their tents.

They were clearly oblivious to what was unfolding steadily around and, in fact, right underneath them.

JJ snored and twitched in his sleep, chasing imaginary rabbits down imagined burrows. He was ignoring the pleas and calls from the girls in his sleep, much as he mostly did when awake.

Lucy was dreaming a strange dream.

In her dream she was dressed in multicoloured clothes, like a crazy morris dancer or one of those Harlequin clowns from the logo of the rugby team Tait's dad Mark supported, covered in frills and patches of rainbow.

She was dancing through the narrow streets of a coastal town, a bit like the beloved Cornish port town of Coverack but with smaller and tighter paths and roads.

She was playing on a flute and as she danced and played, all sorts of animals were joining her. They were just appearing from everywhere, from houses, bushes, hedgerows and paths.

But they weren't ordinary animals. They were exotic

creatures and beasts, like tall giraffes, huge elephants and herds of exotic antelope and deer.

They were following her hypnotic playing and her crazy, crazy jig of a dance.

Outside, back in the real world, it was still that pre-dawn time, crisp with early frost and the kiss of dew on green grass.

In the swampy moat, newts searched for breakfast, hungry mouths agape, while dragonfly larvae darted at tadpoles hiding in the mud.

A fruit bat circled above, its clicking failing to disturb a shiny kingfisher that slept on a perch, ready to catch the first sticklebacks of the morning unawares.

None of the adults stirred.

They were lying on groundsheets millimetres above the meadow that covered the tunnels below. A thin mist licked about their tents and they seemed to have fallen into a very deep sleep indeed.

All around them their children snuggled peacefully in their sleeping bags.

Ordinarily, this would have been a scene of peaceful slumbering bliss.

Yet none of the campers had the slightest notion of the hateful forces heading their way. Nor could they have imagined the horrors that would soon be converging on that ancient, enchanted, fateful spot.

Flying with the breeze at their backs, the wood nymphs made it to the castle ruins before daybreak.

Dianah led them to the highest of the remaining flint ramparts, from where they could survey most of what would originally have been the castle floor, now a lush platform of well-kept lawn.

Tall grasses grew most of the way around the ground, on either side of the raised path that overlooked the moat, much of which was now drained of water. Ducks, coots and moorhens had set up home in the reeds in the deeper areas, doubtless well fed by visiting families.

Several old oak trees had fallen and bridged the moat in certain areas, places where children played during long summer days before storming the last remaining watchtower atop the last intact hill.

Few people ventured here at night, as it was reputed to be haunted by the spirit of the prisoners held then executed here in ancient times. Which is why it came as such a shock to the sprites to see the modest encampment right in the middle of the grounds.

"Humans," said Sylvie, nodding towards the assorted triangle shapes visible through the morning mist.

"Certainly complicates things," pondered Nimbus, looking to Dianah for answers.

She, however, had her head on more pressing matters.

She had noticed the buzzards circling just beneath the cloud line for some time now.

They too were riding the thermals, as the nymphs had, but vertically, rising and falling in the sky as if anticipating a large meal to come and checking when it was likely to arrive.

As if on cue, Alice was the first to notice the light begin to glow and then grow in the tree canopy surrounding the watchtower. It was the same putrid hue that lit up the quarry on the hill.

"Look," said Alice. "It is starting. They are coming."

As the friends watched the glow grow brighter, reflected off the stone walls, from the west a large, dark cloud loomed suddenly larger.

At first, the woodland nymphs feared it may be another aerial threat, until they made out the distinctive flying style of their friends the owls.

The rodents had free rein in the forest that night as it seemed that every barn, eagle and even little owl had rallied to join the faeries of the forest and fly to their aid.

Each bird had given a ride to a nymph or an elf, some clad in wooden armour, and soon hundreds of enchanted folk took up defensive positions of their own.

Soon the ancient walls were lined with razor talons, needle-sharp beaks, slingshots, wands and spears and the night sky was a blur of bats and songbirds answering the rallying call to arms in their own distinctive way. From the north, over the brow of the hill, galloped wave after wave of woodland deer.

First arrived the horned monarchs, then the juvenile bucks before the herds of sinewy does and barking muntjac the size of dogs, all prepared to do what they could for the natural order.

At the lip of the moat, an army of moles, helped by powerful badger clans, busied themselves undermining the grassy banks, creating traps and pitfalls that would slow the enemy down.

While up in the trees, squirrels and wood mice bit through branches preparing perils from above and bees swarmed, buzzing patiently until called into action.

Even the hedgehogs had come in their hundreds, prepared to curl into spiked balls to be fired from miniature machines magically fashioned by the clever gnomes.

Hundreds of thousands of normally peace-loving forest creatures had answered Hearne's emergency call.

Even though they all knew that mankind had faults and many were responsible for the greed and pollution that had created the evil race of creatures marching underground, they also knew what would happen if the peace with the humans was broken.

So they had come to fight with their friends to defend the land they loved and the right of everyone to continue to share it, in peace.

The first sighting of the werebeast army was, as expected, at the top of the tower.

But Hearne's forces held their ground, hoping that sense would prevail and the werewytch would either open talks or back off in the face of overwhelming odds.

Yet the monster mass that trickled down from the top of the tower was nothing like the size the nymphs had seen earlier and, even with a steady flow of hunched horrors, gathering in a mob, they were little more than a single battalion. They were outnumbered and surrounded.

It was then that Dianah's clever strategic eye realised that something was wrong here.

As the forest force tightened around the chattering werebeasts, she suddenly noticed movement around the extreme perimeter of the moat.

She fired a signal flare from her wand but it was largely too late.

Hundreds of bizarre beasts were emerging from the roads the other side of the raised moat.

Clearly there were a number of tunnel exit points and now their enemies streamed over the logs that bridged the moat, flanking then encircling the forces that trapped their decoy army.

The forest force was suddenly caught in two minds

and had to engage on two fronts as first the decoy monsters charged at them and then the screaming beasts smashed into their rear.

Their aerial forces tried valiantly to restore balance and filled the air with a swirling, noisy mass intended to confuse and frighten the enemy.

But their foes were fearless and possessed, snatching starlings, sparrows and robins from the air and crushing them on the run.

The faerie folk sent volley after volley of sharp thorn arrows and spiked hedgehog balls into the charging beasts, forcing them back into the murky moat waters in places.

But there were just too many of them.

Even the monarch bucks with their great antlers scything through rows of the bizarre beasts found their powers blunted when the werewytch appeared on the tower hill and worked her black magic.

To their horror, many of the bucks shed their horns suddenly, something they normally only do in the autumn, so they had to turn to sharp hooves and barging bodies instead. While they gave a powerful account of themselves, she had taken away much of their potency. Even so, many a werebear, badger or wolf met its end as a result of a well-placed kick or determined trample.

Wielding the Willowand, Alice made short work of the last of the decoy force by turning a couple of hives of bees into flying perils the size of cats.

But the problem with bees, whatever their size, is that as soon as they sting they sadly die. So, while effective, it was a trick simply too sad to repeat as the world could not afford to lose too many of their striped kind.

Dianah, meanwhile, jumped from the flint walls onto the back of an eagle owl. Then, followed by a dozen of the bravest nymphs, they flew with stealth and grace towards the tower where the werewytch commanded her force. It was typical of Dianah, running straight at the trouble others run away from.

She signalled for four companions to launch a frontal assault on the wytch, who noticed them coming, as planned, and was drawn into directing a counter-strike by her own raptors.

The aerial fight that followed was well balanced until she intervened and downed two of her opponents with dark spells. But this bought Dianah time.

Before the wytch could react, her own owl had circled behind her and was on her and clawing at her eyes.

Dianah managed to somersault from the bird's back and sank her spear into the wytch's neck, causing her to scream with pain and drop back through the tunnel entrance.

But, just as hope started to rise, a massive werebeast raced from the shadows.

It was Sam.

In the blink of an eye, he pounced at Dianah, hungry for meat.

He caught her off guard and the last her companions saw was the sudden eruption of white feathers that sprang from the beast's snapping jaws.

Word of Dianah's demise, their greatest warrior, soon rippled around the faerie folk, making its way to Alice and Nimbus, who were riding upon the backs of brave deer, darting into and out of the ranks of the monsters, luring them into the traps set by the diggers.

They barely had time to feel sorrow or fear, however, as they were struggling for their own survival.

Snatching a look around the battle ground, Helice, the lord of the nymph folk, could see that they were being squeezed into a tighter and tighter defensive circle by the snarling, snapping, crazed werebeasts.

He summoned a row of archers, who fired swift volleys into a section of the beasts and they then led them on a merry dance back to the moat, creating some brief respite for their encircled friends, much to Sam's howling fury.

Meanwhile, the enchantment spell the girls' father had cast on the tents of the campers still ensured that no-one stirred there. However, the unwitting human families were now right in the centre of battle and nobody knew how long the enchantment would last.

As the dark horde closed ranks yet again, a loud roar and then series of screams and yelps erupted from the rear.

Sylvie could see a gang of around a dozen werebeasts, slightly taller than the rest, led by one with a distinctly thicker and glossier pelt. Incredibly, they soon realised that these werebeasts were savagely attacking the others.

The new creatures were slightly different in that they moved almost upright and used their limbs in attack more than biting jaws. But they were clearly incredibly strong, worked as a close team and were causing mayhem and waves of fear to wash over the enemy unnerved by what appeared to be treacherous betrayal by their own kind.

Sylvie looked up to where the wytch had reappeared, one hand to her neck which now clearly distressed her. The sight of the traitorous werebeasts infuriated her as she could be heard above the hubbub, screaming in anger.

By this stage, the branch traps were raining down on her army. But, with a wave of her arms, accompanied by a bluish light, she appeared to summon a mini whirlwind that whipped around the foot of the hill before picking up the broken branches and hurling them into the fighting crowd.

Her attack hurt and disabled more of her own allies than the enemy. But it succeeded in breaking the line of the backup force, if not their spirit.

Her victory was short-lived, however, as she quickly had to wheel and turn her attention to a new, unanticipated threat.

A series of loud screeches marked the sudden arrival of a most unexpected foe.

Alice noticed the new threat but couldn't believe her eyes, for through the gap in the tree line flew a large mob of emberhawks. But, just as their hearts fell, she noticed something about the lead hawk.

There, riding the same bird that had carried him off earlier, was none other than their fallen friend, Zephyr.

He was clearly unhurt by his ordeal and was now standing proud aboard his feathered steed, firing his bow into the werewytch's minions, accompanied by the rest of the elders, fighting like a creature possessed.

The aerial battle between the emberhawks and the red kites dominated the castle skyline as they darted and slashed, dived and parried with terrible beaks and claws. Some, locked in a terrible dance, plummeted into the wrestling masses on the ground, never to rise again.

But the werewytch had more misery planned.

On her signal, several of her twisted creatures set about burrowing into the banks of the watchtower.

Eventually cracks appeared and a terrible cloud of foul-smelling gas bubbled out, forcing winged creatures from the air and pushing the defensive circle to crumble on the northern edge.

The werebeasts, seemingly unaffected by the foul fumes, roared louder now and started to drive a wedge into the heart of the forest force.

Only the rallying of Helice and the elders provided a countering presence and were it not for a concentrated blast from their wands, which Alice and Nimbus joined, all would have been lost there and then.

To howls of derision from their foes, however, their powerful force field, bounced off the flint and crystal in the castle walls, and shattered before it could do most damage.

Yet their force was much reduced now. Those

isolated by the surge had been compelled to turn and flee. Many were hurt and wounded and others simply exhausted, struggling with a foe driven by a strange power they just didn't understand. Alice and the spellcasters looked especially drained. There was something about this place that was sapping them more than usual.

Shrouded beneath a magical bubble created by Helygenn, the forest folk could at least draw breath and regroup.

Huddled around their elders, what remained of their brave warriors patiently awaited news of their plan while rows of eyes and teeth watched intently and lustily from the dark places.

Helice, nursing a deep gash across his chest, was still gathering his thoughts when the castle walls started to glow with a golden light.

Then they all started to notice a hush that had descended upon the castle; even the werebeasts had fallen silent.

All eyes were gradually drawn towards the south and main gateway close to where a railway bridge now stood.

Various creatures were shuffling aside respectfully, until the mob parted, forming a tunnel of bodies.

Into the midst of this train of anger, walking slowly and regally, the woodland nymphs and forest creatures were shocked to see none other than Hearne, their prince, their monarch, their king.

And alongside him walked a human, a man. He was

instantly recognisable to many of the party as Lord James Trelgathwin, of the Legend of the Lost. He was known by some as James Savage. But he was known, simply, by his children, as their dad.

At first, Holly and Savannah, in their human form, made as if to break through the rainbow shield to join him.

But a simple look and slight shake of his head halted that plan.

The path created by the werebeasts extended from the gate to the watchtower on the hill that the werewytch had commanded since the battle began.

Atop the platform at the crest of the hill, Alice recognised the cauldron Nimbus had liberated from their cabin. It was glowing ominously.

Then her heart dropped when she realised that Nimbus too must have fallen during the battle, a terrible thought confirmed by the fact that her searching eyes couldn't find his normally beaming face in her modest crowd of comrades.

Looking up again, her eyes drawn by the steady procession in front of them, she noticed, with horror, a group of forest folk suspended from the oak tree by a webbing net. Prisoners, clearly caught in a black magic trap.

Hearne and James made their way slowly through the mangy ranks and around the hill until they eventually joined the dark wytch and her entourage near the tunnel entrance.

They appeared to confer for a few brief minutes. Then they all disappeared into the tunnel's black mouth.

"Be brave and hold steady" were the first, comforting words the forest folk heard as Lord Helice, helmet under his arm, flew up and down their ranks.

"This rabble will not hold without their leader. Hold your heads high, friends. We must have faith and bide our time. Look to your companions, your loved ones and your neighbours. We are fighting for our homes, our forest, our glade and our peace. Together we are stronger. We shall win out."

His words were like a warming breeze on a chilly night. Combined with the healing power of the crystal shield, the forest army was recovering fast.

Outside, in the shadows, the werebeasts were starting to bicker and squabble with one another.

Without the werewytch, the dark hold over them was waning and fights were starting to break out in their ranks as fear and doubt, confusion and hunger crept in.

Around the fringes of their massed circle, creatures started to drift away and slink off into what was left of the night.

But then, heralded by a great cloud of darkly luminescent bats and a roar like broken thunder, the werewytch reappeared atop the hill. Even from a distance, she seemed taller and bolder now than ever.

Then, to the horror of the forest clan, she held aloft the ultimate trophy of them all.

There, raised in her malicious fist, she held the antlers of the monarch of the forest kingdom and the collective cry from his people shamed the dawn.

"Now!" was all that Helice had to utter as a battle cry, such was their collective anger.

Suddenly, every enraged forest creature, minibeast, bird, rodent and faerie folk charged, the rainbow shield shattering into a trillion shards of bright light that hit the mewling mob of werebeasts like sharp darts of goodness.

Those hit by the force of light simply fell where they stood, while those behind them were so distracted by the flashing light that they barely resisted the charge.

Soon, whole ranks of distorted beasts were falling down the banks into the moat, where all manner of aquatic creatures set about them.

"Now!" was a cry repeated by Nelson, who appeared just beyond the moat as dozens of gypsy pirates ran across the tree bridges wielding swords, pikes, clubs and guns.

They tore up the banks of the watchtower, forcing the werewytch to send Sam and her close bodyguard down the hill in the hope of heading them off.

But Holly came with her own dark, winged army and the biggest of the werebeasts were soon preoccupied with fending off hundreds of clutching and scraping claws and stabbing beaks, defeating bulk with weight of numbers.

In the watery moat, Savannah's friends were fast rounding up the shivering, whimpering creatures in large groups, pinning them in a swampy area very difficult to navigate on foot.

Alice, meanwhile, had her own mission to complete. While her friends were fighting for their homes and friends, her own head was spinning.

For everything she had taken for granted about herself and her little family had been shaken from root to branch.

She was upset, she was angry and she needed answers. Now only one person had them.

Darting between dive-bombing bats and ploughing through a flock of angry jays with strange glowing eyes, using sharp power bursts from the Willowand to knock them from the air, she headed along the lip of the moat towards the hill her mother occupied.

Meanwhile, approaching from the opposite direction, was the sinewy sight of Henry, but in werebeast form.

He too wanted answers but, having lost many of his peace-loving friends in this battle, he not only wanted an explanation; he wanted to vent a great deal of pain.

Most of the werebeasts left him alone, their minds too twisted by whatever possessed them to understand that he wasn't one of them.

The forest folk, however, could barely distinguish friend from foe either so he had to be fast and move in the shadows.

Holly too was on a mission.

She had seen her father disappear into that dark tunnel and was becoming increasingly desperate for she had not seen him, or Hearne, return and she feared the worst.

Wrapped in the Rubyrobe, she barrelled and twisted as she flew, like a scarlet bullet.

Anything that attempted to bite, sting or strike her simply couldn't find their target as she sped towards the top of the mound.

Meanwhile, the Ravenring continued to conjure shadows, illusions and tricks of the light creating the impression that their army had many more troops than it did.

Holly flew above a gang of gypsy pirates, led by the irrepressible Ziggy, who, she saw, handled a cutlass with great skill.

They were holding their own against twice as many of the monsters and creating space and time for what came next.

Alice arrived before the werewytch first and had changed to her mortal shape without breaking her momentum.

At first her mother, her face now twisted with an emotion she hadn't seen before, raised her hands as if to strike her daughter.

"How dare you approach..." she gasped, but choked down on her words as Alice met her gaze and simply cried, "Why?"

Before she could come to terms with her daughter's stinging words, her son browed the hill.

He held the unconscious form of Sam in his strong arms. His face was rapidly shrinking and transforming from beast to boy.

He said nothing, however, but simply placed his former friend down gently and then walked to his sister's side, not once taking his eyes from his mother's.

Holly's arrival on the hilltop platform, partially sheltered by the remains of the ancient flint wall, incurred a different reaction from the werewytch, however.

Her attention was immediately drawn, not only to the unmistakable similarity between Holly's looks and those of her children, but to the cloak about her shoulders and then the ring glowing dark on her finger.

She suddenly, and for the first time since the battle began, looked terrified.

But, before anyone could move, or even summon up a sentence, the wytch threw the antlers she had held in one hand into the smouldering cauldron.

Within seconds, the temperature dropped, the light breeze turned to a strong westerly wind and thunder shattered the silence.

Flashes of lightning lit up the night sky and it suddenly started to rain, then hail.

A bolt of lightning tore through the darkness.

It struck the oak above them and, as they dived for cover the wytch disappeared into the darkness, screaming.

Something woke Lucy from her deep, enchanted sleep.

It was the sound of a long, guttural scream in a voice she somehow remembered.

No sooner did she wake but she became aware of the noises of battle just the other side of the delicate canvas tent wall.

So it took quite an act of courage for the little girl to tentatively unzip the entrance flap and exit the tent cocoon with her tiny terrier in tow.

As she ran to the castle wall, her senses were suddenly exploding with the sights, sounds and smells of the epic struggle.

Groups of mangy beasts, the like of which she had only ever seen in nightmares, fought with what looked like balls of bright light.

Up above, all manner of flying creature filled the sky, raining feathers with the hail as the storm grew in strength. And the very water seemed to be alive.

Instinctively, she made for higher ground to try and get above the chaos and attempt to make some sense of it all.

She was also keen to find her father, who must have come out to see what was going on, she thought.

Then she realised that she could no longer see the tents where she was sure they were pitched.

Scrambling up the grassy bank on all fours, she was almost at the top when she heard something horrible behind her.

Not stopping to look, she doubled her efforts but it was catching up to her and she could now feel the ground vibrating as it closed in.

Suddenly, Jack the terrier hurtled towards the dark creature and, as she opened her mouth in panic to stop him, what felt like a jet of water arched in the air and slammed into whatever was following her.

Despite lying prone, her arms over her head, she heard it cry out as it fell off the mound. Then a reassuring voice, like gently lapping water, filled her ears.

"Hello, Lucy. We knew you were somewhere close."

Savannah placed her hand upon Lucy's shoulder and helped her to her feet. Then together they climbed the last few steps where the others had gathered.

"Look who I found," said Savannah to Holly, who instantly threw her arms around her sister.

Alice was just starting to realise that there was something very special about this group of children when Henry, now back in boy form, pointed at her, his mouth open.

The small group was glowing silver in the last of the moonlight.

The Moonstone necklace Savannah wore now connected to the Willowand with a light that crackled like an electric charge. This, in turn, connected to

Holly's Rubyrobe, which shimmered and hummed and, lastly, the light ran down her arm to Lucy, who found that, somehow, the Ravenring had passed from her sister's hand to her own.

The group was now connected by a silver diamond of light.

They smiled at each other, realising that the legend had been right and recognising what this now meant for each of them.

They were back, reconnected as siblings, almost a family.

But perhaps most touching of all was Henry, who found himself in the middle.

He had never felt so complete, so alive, so loved, so belonging and it was moving him to tears of quiet, tender joy.

One of the gravest mistakes people make in life is to assume that people are all good or all bad.

The truth is that sometimes bad things happen to people we thought of as good and great things can happen to those we formerly considered evil.

With this in mind, now consider the fate of the werewytch and her twisted army.

They only existed because of some very ill-judged behaviour by some very greedy people who should have known better.

The storm that caused the people of Mousehole to cast the Trelgathwin family afloat had been brought about by their grandmother's evil jealousy, which had twisted and corrupted nature. And who knows what had happened to her or where that evil bubbled up from to poison the old woman's mind?

The seas were so angry with her that they foamed and raged and swallowed the family whole before spitting them out on different shores.

But, had it not been for her magical powers, the abilities they inherited from her, the children would most likely never have found each other again.

Even the battle that still raged here, in the old home of the Black Prince, was happening for a reason.

Had the wicked people who ran the mine that created the poisonous quarry in the hills cared for nature properly, they would have nurtured, not exploited, it and returned it to its original state.

They certainly would not have left the hateful chemicals that harmed the land and so corrupted the animals that the werebeasts were formed.

People may blame the wytch for the war and destruction. But could she really be hated for trying to defend the same land the faerie folk and humans held dear? After all, they were blissfully ignoring a problem she and her kind had to live with, daily.

Yet now, as the children felt the power of the magical diamond surge over them, it became obvious that the war raging around them was clearly no solution to their troubles.

Neither side was giving ground, despite the filthy conditions; both were flagging and casualties were mounting on both sides.

But would anyone really claim victory, this night? With so many casualties, could either side triumph?

As if to answer this question, the children soon became conscious of a low rumbling within the tunnel in the hill.

It grew from a quiet thunder to what sounded like a series of bellows, roaring and then trumpeting, which to Lucy's mind could only mean one thing.

Her dream in Mermaid Cottage. It was coming to life.

Somehow they had heard their summons and another force was answering nature's call.

The rest of the animals were on their way; they were coming.

What burst into the castle clearing then was a truly bizarre sight. For soon, every form of beast of the African plains, Asian jungles or American drifts charged through the tunnel exit and down into the castle grounds.

Stunned at the sight of lions, zebra, hippo and buffalo, galloping alongside tigers, apes, lions and oryx, both warring factions stopped in their tracks, mouths agape.

Soon, it was impossible to raise an arm, wand or fist in anger as the area was alive with the sights and sounds of nature at its wildest, richest and finest and ill will gave way to awe.

Bringing up the rear of this fantastical herd was James, the children's father, riding upon a horned rhino (it didn't look very comfortable).

Better still, Nimbus sat on his shoulder, looking like the cat that just got the cream.

"Should have known he would steal our glory," laughed Zephyr, untangling himself from the reeds a werebear had swatted him into just moments before.

He then flew to embrace his best friend enthusiastically.

Raising their arms as one, the children on the hill sent their magical diamond of light straight up into the air.

Here it blended with the clouds and brought the storm to an abrupt end.

Then, arm in arm, supporting each other's weary

souls that had been through such terribly tough times, they walked down the hill to join their father and their friends.

All around them, the werebeasts appeared to be, for want of a better phrase, thawing out.

The wretched smoke had all but disappeared and the ugly luminescence had gone from the horizon.

As they recovered from the effects of the storm, the deep glow in their eyes faded and their bodies seemed to straighten and gradually change.

Eventually, werebadgers looked more like simple badgers again, wereweasels lost the were, and so on.

Foes they had fought just minutes before greeted them like long-lost friends. And it all happened so fast yet so gradually; it's hard to explain.

By now, the gypsy pirate clan had gathered around their true leader.

They were admittedly a little wary of his unconventional steed and the creatures surrounding him. But all laughed when a wiry terrier appeared from nowhere and started nibbling at the heels of the prehistoric beast.

James and Nelson in particular, embraced like the closest of friends.

"The animals of Whipsnade. So that's what my dream was all about," muttered Lucy to herself, as she smiled at the scenes around her, the Ravenring still tingling on her index finger.

She then bent down to take JJ's lickyness as he worked his way round the children in turn.

But then Lucy noticed Alice, sitting all on her own, her back to the old castle keep, shoulders hunched.

So she wandered over.

"What's wrong, my sister? Aren't you happy that our memories have returned now and we've all found each other again?"

"Found each other?" snapped Alice. "I didn't even know I was lost. I didn't ask for this terrible fight and... and..."

"What about our mother?" said Holly, who had just joined them.

"You're worried about her, the wytch?"

"But you didn't even know her. I did. We lived together in that cabin for a very long time.

"She isn't an evil person.

"She isn't the wytch people say she is, even though..." gasped Alice, feeling her temper rise and cheeks and neck redden.

"Even though she started this war?" said the voice of the man she now remembered to be her long-lost and much-missed father.

At the sound of his voice, Alice burst into uncontrollable sobs.

"But now she's gone. We've destroyed her."

There followed a few moments of uncomfortable but necessary silence while James simply held his young daughter tight in his arms for the first time in, oh, too long a time.

They hugged each other until the worst of the ache in their bones had thawed like ice.

She may have had her mother's looks, but in so many ways she had his passion, stamina and pride.

His heart swelled at the way she was standing up for his partner, despite the mess the enchanted madness made.

But just then a quiet voice broke through the crying.

"Don't be sad, darling. I haven't gone anywhere."

When she looked up through watery eyes, she was greeted by not just the strong, kind smile of her father or the now-liberated, peaceful face of her mother but the loving eyes of her siblings too.

For this, above all, was her own, special family. Then, high on the hill that led from the castle to the forest to the Chalk Downs, a golden noise rang out as Hearne sounded his great horn.

He was signalling another dawn.
He was announcing another day.
He was heralding a fresh beginning.

ABOUT THE AUTHOR

English author Ian P Buckingham is widely published across a range of genres and mediums. A bit of a modern renaissance man, his work spans high-brow business books on brand and communication as well as magical adventure stories for children and young adults.

Winner of various creative writing prizes throughout his career and education in Africa and England, he has studied at Harvard as well as the University of Leeds where he also specialised in children's and Commonwealth literature.

Ian has edited several publications including poetry and creative writing magazines and has written, produced and directed plays. A proud father of two daughters (the muses for the important work) and a passionate shared parenting advocate, when not writing or roaming Britain's coastline and forests, Ian is a prominent management consultant and MBA lecturer, championing the crucial role of great stories in life generally, no matter the age of the reader.

For details of our other books, or to submit
your own manuscript please visit
www.green-cat.co

GREEN CAT BOOKS

Printed in Great Britain
by Amazon

71832724R00137